I0570371

REAPER

EDWARD KENDRICK

Reaper
ISBN # 978-1-78430-822-3
©Copyright Edward Kendrick 2015
Cover Art by Posh Gosh ©Copyright October 2015
Interior text design by Claire Siemaszkiewicz
Pride Publishing

Published in 2015 by Pride Publishing, Newland House, The Point, Weaver Road, Lincoln, LN6 3QN, United Kingdom.

Pride Publishing is a subsidiary of Totally Entwined Group Limited.

REAPER

Dedication

To my family

Chapter One

"Get behind me, kid," Reaper ordered. When the obviously homeless teen seemed ready to argue, Reaper pointed to the two toughs coming toward them down the dark street. "You want to deal with them, be my guest."

The teen swallowed hard as he did what Reaper had told him.

"Looking for trouble, boys?" Reaper asked, his arms crossed over his chest.

The larger, muscular punk sneered. "You gonna give it to us, old man?"

"Try me and see."

The smaller guy pounded the bat he was holding on the ground while the bigger one tossed a knife from hand to hand. Then they attacked. Reaper grabbed the bat as it swung toward his head, twisting it out of the punk's grip. Then he used it to break the wrist of the knife-wielding assailant, smiling when the punk's scream shattered the relative silence.

"Next time — well, there's not going to be a next time, is there, boys?" Reaper said, looking at them with contempt. "You" — he jabbed a finger at the smaller of the pair — "get your buddy out of here before I decide to do some real damage." He held up the bat, eyeing the one he was talking to. "Maybe a couple of blows to your thick skulls will teach you to stop preying on street kids who can't defend themselves."

"Who the hell are you?" the muscular teen asked, his words a mixture of pain and defiance as he held his broken wrist to his chest with his free hand.

"The name's Reaper. And I'm someone who doesn't like thugs like you going after kids like him." Reaper glanced behind himself and shook his head. "Guess he decided to find a safer place to be while he had the chance. You might want to as well." He bent, keeping an eye on the smaller guy as he picked up the fallen knife. "Nice one. I think I'll hang on to it. Now, beat it. Oh, you might want to see a doctor about your wrist."

The punks took off.

The injured one called back, "You're going to regret this."

Probably not. Reaper moved into the closest alley, broke the bat over the edge of a dumpster and tossed the pieces into it.

How the hell could he afford this? Reaper folded the knife, clipping it to his belt. He knew it cost well over a hundred and fifty bucks, if bought legally. *But then, considering what he planned on doing with it, he probably stole it.*

Reaper went back to the sidewalk, keeping an eye open for any more trouble. He came to another alley and glanced down it to make sure everything was normal. Well, as normal as seeing kids and adults huddled in doorways or behind dumpsters could be. He moved on, the false dawn beginning to lighten the sky ahead of him.

* * * *

"Mr. Ward, your next appointment is here," Ms. Burke, Zack's secretary, said. She stood in the doorway to his office.

"Please show him in, Alice." When his secretary did, Zack stood and crossed the room, to greet the older man. "A pleasure to see you again, Mr. Rawlins. Please have a seat."

After his client was seated, Zack returned to his own chair and they began discussing Mr. Rawlins' investments. Zack suggested a few changes that would bolster the man's retirement account, and twenty minutes later, he was ushering Mr. Rawlins out of the office.

The rest of Zack's day continued on in the same vein, either with personal meetings with his clients, or with phone calls to them. As a respected investment counselor, his client list included some of the wealthier members of the community, as well as those with smaller incomes who wanted to have money to retire on when the time came.

Zack made a good living at what he did, as evidenced by his house. He looked at it with appreciation now while he waited for the barred entrance gate in the high stone walls surrounding the property to open. When it did, he went through, closed it again and drove up the driveway to the attached garage.

It was more house than he probably needed, but it suited his desire for privacy. And there was a panoramic view of the Rockies from the second floor balcony that kept him from feeling as if he was imprisoned within the confines of his well-secured estate.

He unlocked the door from the garage to the kitchen and inhaled the aroma coming from the kitchen. "Pot roast. Mrs. Cook must have read my mind." It amused him that the cook-slash-housekeeper's name was Cook. If he was honest with himself—and he usually was—her name was one of the reasons he'd hired her. That and her ability to make fantastic meals and keep the house clean—and do it all before she left at two.

Walking through the living room and the recreation room, he then went upstairs to his bedroom.

After kicking off his shoes and hanging up his suit coat, he stepped out on the balcony to watch the late afternoon sun silhouetting the mountains. "Another beautiful evening," he murmured. "But then they usually are this time of year." He spent a few minutes savoring the view then went back inside to change into jeans and a comfortable, well-worn work shirt before going back downstairs to eat.

I swear, Mrs. Cook has it in for me. I bet I put on ten pounds, as good as that was. He chuckled, knowing he'd work it off. He always did. After he finished, he washed the dishes then mixed a drink, picked up the book he was reading and went out onto the rear patio to enjoy the cool early evening. An hour later, he was back upstairs, where he showered then went to bed.

* * * *

Reaper walked down the dark streets on high alert for potential trouble. The bars had closed less than fifteen minutes earlier and the patrons—some drunk, some relatively sober—were heading to their cars or roaming the area in search of something more to keep them occupied.

He saw three young men, obviously very intoxicated, huddled together, watching two young women entering a parking lot. As the trio began to follow them, Reaper stepped into their path.

"If I were you," he told the oldest one, "I'd call a cab for you and your friends and go home to your wives. Assuming any woman would be stupid enough to marry you."

He got the reaction he'd wanted as the men forgot their intended targets to focus on him.

"What do you mean, stupid enough?" one of the trio said, fisting his hands.

"Exactly what it sounded like. Look at you. You all smell like a brewery. If I hadn't seen you coming out of the bar, I'd figure you spent the night sharing a bottle of rotgut behind a dumpster."

"Motherfucker! Where do you get off talking to us like that?" one of them said, taking a swing at Reaper.

Reaper caught his arm and shoved him into the second man, who seemed intent on rushing him. They went down in a heap, leaving just the largest man to be dealt with. Apparently being large did not equate with being reckless. The man took one look at his companions, turned tail and fled.

Reaper glanced at the parking lot and saw a car with the women in it pulling out onto the street. Figuring they were safe now from their intended assailants—as was anyone else in the neighborhood—he pulled the two drunks to their feet, gripping their arms tightly. He pushed them face first against the brick wall of a nearby building, their arms now twisted behind their backs. "Next time you even think about going after defenseless women, remember I could be somewhere close by. Got that?"

"Bastard," one of them swore angrily.

Reaper chuckled. "I am, and don't you forget it. Now get the hell out of here before I do you some serious damage." He smiled tightly as the two men hotfooted it away without looking back.

"You did a good job there," someone said from behind Reaper. "But you should have left it to us."

Reaper turned to see who was speaking. A patrol car had pulled up to the curb, the motor still running. The officer riding shotgun looked him over, shaking his head. "We don't condone vigilantes." He held out his hand, saying, "Your ID, please."

"Me, Officer" — Reaper peered at his nametag while digging his wallet out of his pocket — "Comstock? I was just defending myself from a couple of drunks."

"Right. Looked more like you were trying to teach them a lesson from where we were standing Mister..." The officer looked the driver's license when Reaper took it out of his wallet. "Mister Wallace."

Reaper chuckled when he heard the other officer say, "Well, technically sitting, but who's going to quibble about semantics?"

"Not me," Reaper said. "And if you were so concerned, why didn't you help me?"

"You seemed to have things well under control," the officer who'd first spoken replied. He handed back the license. "I'm serious, though. Those three were not interested in you until you got in their faces."

Reaper nodded. "They were after two women who left the bar just before they did. So I figured..." He shrugged.

"You'd play the hero. Like I said, next time, call us. That's what *we* get paid to do."

"Got it," Reaper replied, giving them a mock salute before turning and walking off.

He continued on his self-appointed rounds after the cops had moved on. Sure, he'd dealt with those drunks, since they obviously had intentions of doing something to the two women. But Reaper was much more interested in protecting street kids and the homeless from the creeps who preyed on them. He'd lived on the streets himself twenty years ago and knew what it was like and what the dangers were. If it hadn't been for the man who had rescued him and showed him there were better options, he figured he'd still be one of the people sleeping in alleys and selling drugs — or his body — to keep from starving to death.

Now he was paying it forward — championing those who were weak and unable to defend themselves — against the punks, pimps and dealers who seemed to make it their business to beat them down, literally as well as figuratively.

* * * *

"We should have arrested him," Mike said, as he put the squad car in gear.

"For what?" Dallas asked. "Teaching a trio of drunks to behave themselves? No harm, no foul, and from what he said, he stopped them from potentially assaulting a couple of females."

"If he was telling the truth."

"Guess we'll never know one way or the other."

"One thing for sure, he probably wasn't bar-hopping," Mike said as he pulled the car out onto the street. "Not in leathers. There are no biker bars around here. Makes me wonder if what you said was the truth. Maybe he *is* playing vigilante."

"With that build and the way he handled himself, could be. He wasn't armed, though."

"How do you know?"

Dallas snorted. "I checked him out? A knife? Yeah, he could have had one in his boot or the small of his back under the vest, I guess."

"Maybe you should have frisked him," Mike said with a knowing grin.

"If we run into him again, maybe I will," Dallas replied, laughing.

* * * *

An hour later, Reaper walked along a street where he knew some of the teenaged girls hung out waiting for johns willing to pay for a quick blow job. A car pulled up beside one of them and the driver rolled down the window. The girl went over, shaking her head a moment later at something he said then nodding. She looked wary but went around to the other side of the car and opened the door. Seconds later, she was being dragged into the car.

The Reaper recognized the man for what he was—a local small-time pimp. So, without hesitation, he moved swiftly to stop the driver before he could take off, pulling his knife from its sheath at the back of his waist. The driver must have seen him coming in the side view mirror because he put the car in gear. Reaper grabbed the edge of the window frame with one hand, slashing the knife blade across the man's arm. The man howled in pain. Feeling like a pirate for a moment, Reaper gripped the hilt of the knife in his teeth then reached down and opened the door. Before the man could react, Reaper pulled him out of the car.

"Step on the brake," he ordered the terrified girl. It took her a moment to clamber over the console and stamp down, hard, bringing the car to a stop.

Meanwhile, Reaper dragged the man to his feet then knocked him out with a hard uppercut to his jaw. Ignoring the cheers from the girls watching, he threw the man over his shoulder, strode down to a dumpster and tossed him into it. Then, with a bow to his audience, he continued on his way.

* * * *

"We have an interesting one," Dallas said after answering the dispatcher's call. "Looks like our vigilante might have struck again." He told Mike where, and within five minutes, they were pulling up to an alley. An ambulance was already there, and when they joined the EMTs, they found them ministering to a man who had a deep cut across his left forearm. He had also, quite obviously, been pulled out of the dumpster at the end of the alley.

"How is he?" Dallas asked one of the EMTs.

"He lost a fair amount of blood and has a fractured jaw, but he'll live."

"Any witnesses to what happened?" Dallas asked, looking at a small group of teenaged girls huddled together at the edge of the alley.

They seemed hesitant to talk, not too surprising in Dallas' opinion, given the location. It was a known spot for girls trying to sell themselves to make enough money to stay alive.

Finally, one of them stepped forward. "That bastard tried to grab Jinx. Then this dude comes out of nowhere and stops him. Tossed him in there"—she pointed to the dumpster—"like the trash he is then vanished."

"Describe him, please," Dallas said, taking notes.

"Tall. Way tall. Like six foot, maybe."

Dallas tried not to smile. Given that the girl was probably five-four at best, he could see why she'd said that.

"He was all in black. Leather pants, turtleneck, a vest, I think, although it could have been a jacket. Hard to tell 'cause it was dark. His hair was sorta long and…shaggy? He had a knife for sure."

"Which one is Jinx?" Mike asked.

The girl shook her head. "Not telling."

"Look, we're not going to arrest her. I just want her side of the story."

"Uh-huh. Heard that one before."

A skinny girl dressed in short shorts and a tight T-shirt stepped forward. "I'm Jinx." She held out her arm. "He did this when he grabbed me." There were deep bruises on her wrist and one on her forehead.

He pointed to her face, asking, "Did he hit you?"

"Naw. My head hit the edge of the door when he pulled me into the car." Suddenly she started shaking. One of the other girls quickly wrapped an arm around her. "He…he was going to…" Jinx whispered. "If it wasn't for that man…"

"You were lucky he showed up," Dallas said.

"Yeah, 'cause for sure there weren't no cops around," another girl muttered.

Dallas cocked his head but refused to fall into a debate with her about what she'd said.

By then the EMTs had the man on a gurney and were putting him into the ambulance. Mike was with them, taking down the man's particulars.

Dallas asked Jinx for her real name, knowing it was a fruitless question, even though he pointed out he'd need it and an address if they were going to file charges against the man for his attempted abduction. "I'll also need you to come down to the station house to make a statement and sign it."

"No way," Jinx said with a hard shake of her head. Obviously having regained some of her confidence, she muttered, "I'm not stupid. I tell you who I am, you call my folks and the shit hits the fan again."

"We'll have to let him go if you don't," Dallas pointed out. "Then he might come looking for you."

Jinx glanced at the other girls. The older one who had first told Dallas what had happened put her arm around Jinx's shoulders. "He won't try again, thanks to the dude in black."

"Reaper," the youngest-looking one whispered.

"What?" Dallas asked, turning to her.

"Reaper. There are stories going around about a man who…who takes care of us when something bad goes down. I bet that was him. He's called Reaper."

Arching an eyebrow at Mike, who had joined him now, Dallas said, "That's a new one on me."

"Yeah, me too. When we get back to the station, let's see if anyone else has heard of him or filed any reports involving someone called The Reaper. At least we have his real name, if that was him earlier tonight."

"And if his ID was legit." Dallas returned his attention to the girls. "Is there anything else you can tell us about The Reaper?"

"Not *The* Reaper. Just Reaper," the one who'd mentioned him said.

One of the others nodded. "I know a dude he saved from a beating about a week ago. According to him, Reaper told the bastard to remember his name, because if he tried anything like that again, he'd be hearing it in his nightmares after Reaper was done with him."

"A bit melodramatic," Mike muttered.

"Probably effective, though. Okay, ladies, unless there's something you forgot to tell us, we're finished here." Dallas stared at them one by one, focusing finally on Jinx. "I know it's rough out here and you're doing the only thing you think you can to survive. But remember...next time you might not be so lucky." He smiled wryly. "I shouldn't be saying this, but find a couple of guys to hang with you when you're out here. It'll make the johns think twice about trying to pull what that asshole did tonight."

One of the girls giggled. "Cops aren't supposed to talk like that."

"Hey, we're human too," Mike said, smiling. "We call it as we see it and that SOB was an asshole."

"He was, so please think about what I said." Dallas told them before going back to the squad car with Mike.

As they drove away, Dallas sighed. "They won't, of course."

"Probably not," Mike agreed. "And now they'll be trusting that this Reaper guy will show up to save them if they run into trouble again."

"Which he probably won't. Even if he's doing what they think—protecting street kids—he can't be everywhere all the time any more than we can."

"Too true. Too true."

* * * *

It was seven-thirty in the morning. Zack smiled when he heard footsteps on the stairs to the second floor. He finished drying his hair, wrapped a towel around his waist and stepped out of the bathroom just as Dallas came into the bedroom.

"You look beat," Zack told him, crossing the room to kiss his lover.

"Thanks to you," Dallas replied with a chuckle. "You did a number on the SOB who tried to abduct that girl. I especially liked the fact he ended up in a dumpster."

"I figured it was fitting, given that he's the kind of bastard who preys on girls. Well, all the kids who are in her position."

"I know," Dallas replied with a sigh of frustration. "It's finding proof against them that's a problem. The girls, and the guys, are too afraid to talk."

"Tell me about it," Zack said angrily as he started to unbutton Dallas' shirt. "Did Mike buy that you don't know me?"

"He did. It was just dumb luck we were there when you took on those drunks. And what was with that anyway?"

Zack smiled ruefully. "I was only doing my usual thing—keeping an eye out for anyone who thought they'd like to hassle the kids who crash in the alleys around the bars in the area. There's been a rash of them being beaten up, as you well know."

With his shirt now unbuttoned, Dallas nodded as he took it off and folded it to put with the other uniforms he had to take to the cleaners before going in to work that evening. "We do the best we can to keep it from happening, but when the kids won't say anything unless they end up in the hospital…" He shrugged then kicked off his shoes and stripped off his pants, adding them to the pile.

"Thus Reaper was born." Zack wrapped his arms around Dallas, kissing him quite thoroughly. "Go shower, and hurry if you want to play around before I have to leave for work."

"Play around?" Dallas grinned. "I call it making love."

Zack hugged him then swatted his butt to get him moving. "There's definitely love involved. However…"

"I know. I'm going." He raked his gaze over Zack. "You couldn't have waited twenty minutes so we could have showered together?"

"Considered it, but the bed is much more comfortable."

"Men," Dallas grumbled before going into the bathroom and closing the door behind him.

Zack laughed. "I know. Can't live with them. Can't live without them."

The fact that Dallas lived with him was a detail known to only four people—Zack, Dallas, Mrs. Cook and one other. Mrs. Cook kept it to herself because she adored both men and understood that Dallas could lose his job if anyone found out he didn't live within the confines of the city. A requirement, he'd explained, for all of the city's police officers. Dallas did have a small apartment downtown that was his official address. However, he rarely used it unless something kept him working overtime. Then, with Zack already on his way to or at his office, Dallas would crash there instead of making the half-hour drive home.

When Dallas came out of the bathroom fifteen minutes later, he hadn't even bothered with the towel, so Zack was able to admire his lover's well-muscled body as Dallas came over to the bed. Zack held out his arms, and Dallas immediately crawled onto the bed and into them.

They kissed for a few moments while using their hands to explore well-known parts of each other's body. Then, since Zack had to leave—way too soon, in his estimation—and Dallas needed to sleep after his twelve-hour shift, they got down to business, minus condoms since they had been together long enough that they didn't need them.

Dallas turned, presenting his hard cock for Zack's eager mouth to enfold, then he took Zack's throbbing, leaking member between his lips. Soon enough, they were thoroughly involved in pleasuring each other. Zack was the expert at deep-throating, while Dallas used his lips and tongue to torment his lover to the peak of ecstasy. Too soon — as much as he tried to ride the pleasure Dallas was giving him — Zack exploded, filling Dallas' mouth with his cum. Even as he did, he swallowed Dallas' cock, knowing his groans of fulfillment would drive his lover over the edge into a full-blown orgasm.

"I swear," Dallas murmured after they'd come down and released each other, "this way is as good as or better than fucking."

Zack smiled, turning so that he could wrap his lover in a tight embrace. "True, when time is at a premium. But" — he tapped Dallas' nose — "I have no intention of giving up long, slow lovemaking that involves getting screwed into oblivion."

"Well, when you put it that way..." Dallas kissed him gently.

"I don't want to leave," Zack grumbled after returning the kiss. "I'd rather hold you while you sleep."

"And get some sleep yourself," Dallas said. "You — "

Zack kissed Dallas again to silence him. He knew what he was going to say. It was a discussion they'd had often enough before. Zack did get six hours sleep between coming home from work and leaving again around one a.m. to make his rounds of the parts of the city where the homeless kids and adults hung out. Dallas wanted him to come home before dawn so that he could at least sleep for another hour or two. Zack tried to do that, but it wasn't always possible.

"Sunday," Zack told Dallas when he finished kissing him. "You're off. I'm off. We can spend the whole day in bed."

"Promise?"

"Yes, love, I promise." Zack grinned wickedly. "I'm not sure we'll get any sleep, though."

With a laugh, Dallas replied, "That works."

* * * *

"You're late," Alice chastised when Zack came into the waiting room of his office suite.

"Sorry. Traffic."

"At nine a.m.?" she asked, lifting one finely arched eyebrow in disbelief.

"There was an accident on the highway." He took off his coat, hung it in the closet then came over to her desk. "Besides which, unless I've gotten my days mixed up, I don't have an appointment until nine-thirty."

"You didn't. Tomorrow, though" — she tapped her computer screen — "you have a nine o'clock."

"I'll set my alarm half an hour earlier, then."

He went into his office and found the folder he needed for his client already laid out in the center of his desk. Not that he was surprised. Alice always seemed to be one step ahead of him when it came to things like that. It was why he'd hired her several years ago, and why she was still working for him to this day. He scanned through it then brought up the pertinent information about the man's investments on his computer, just in time for her to announce that Mr. Collins had arrived.

After they exchanged greetings and both men were seated, Mr. Collins got straight to the point. "I've been talking to the vice-president of Rice and Marshall.

They're planning to purchase the block bounded by First, Second, King and Prince Streets. I need to know your opinion on whether I should buy stock in the company, based on the fact that they intend to tear down the existing buildings and erect a high-rise condominium complex there."

Zack nodded. "So I've heard. I'll have to do some research, of course, but my initial instinct, based on what I know of them, is to hold off until everything is finalized. The people in the neighborhood have mounted a protest over the height of the buildings that could affect R&M's chances of getting the required zoning permits, despite the fact that the company appears to have the zoning board in their pocket at the moment."

"That's what I've been told too, which is why I wanted your input. If the deal does go through, their stock could appreciate immensely."

"And if it doesn't, it could tank." Zack clicked on a website then told Mr. Collins, "At the moment, their stock is holding steady and has been for the last week. It went up slightly on news of their plans, but not enough to jump on it yet."

"Then I'll hold off. Now, about…"

They went on to discuss some of his other investments, with Zack suggesting he sell one stock and put the money into another that had the potential to bring in a steadier, if slower, return with less chance of the price falling as the market fluctuated.

Mr. Collins gave his okay, he and Zack dealt with the paperwork involved, then Collins left.

As soon as Mr. Collins was out of earshot, Zack swore softly. He knew all about the piece of property R&M was working to get their hands on. It was in a rundown area on the edge of the Uptown district that was slowly being gentrified. The block in question held Off-the-Street, one of the city's few homeless shelters. If the shelter closed, there would be more kids on the streets at night, easy prey for the punks who got their jollies beating up on them. And also prey to men like the one last night who went after young teens, mainly the girls, for more than just down-and-dirty sex.

Maybe it's time to start focusing my attention on them. And... He tapped a finger pensively on his lips. *I'll see what I can do about coming up with a new building for the shelter.*

Chapter Two

Reaper moved down the dark streets, searching for the girls he'd met the previous night. He knew that, despite the fact they should know better now, they were probably in the same area. It was a known spot for johns looking for fast, cheap sex.

He discovered he was right when he saw three of them hovering on the stoop of a derelict building. As he neared them, a car pulled up. The oldest of the girls walked over, squatted and talked to the driver. Then, with a nod, she went around the car and got in. Her head disappeared from view, and Reaper knew she was servicing the john. Not too much later, she was back on the street, pocketing the money she'd earned, and the car drove off.

As Reaper approached the girls, he got tentative smiles from them.

"You're the dude from last night," the oldest looking one said.

He nodded.

"Thank you for…being there."

Again, he nodded.

"You're the strong, silent type, aren't you?"

Reaper smiled. "Sometimes." He joined the two other girls on the stoop just as another car approached. "Ignore him," he told the girls. "We need to talk." He could tell the oldest one wanted to disregard his words. "Please. This is more important than a couple more dollars in your pocket."

"Says you," she retorted, but she came over to where they stood.

"To start with, would you tell me your names?" He chuckled softly. "That's make it easier than my calling you Blondie or Shorty."

"I'm Raven," the tallest one said. "'Cause of my hair."

"I'm Star," the youngest one murmured.

"A pretty name," Reaper told her. "And you?" He looked at the last girl, who was about Raven's age, he thought.

She shrugged. "Nickie. I don't have a street name. You do, though. You're Reaper."

"That I am."

"You're famous."

"Good Lord, I hope not."

"You are to us," Raven told him. "You protect us."

"I try to." He leaned back against the side of the building, his gaze moving from girl to girl. "I could use your help, though."

"Us?" Star looked at him in disbelief.

"Yeah, you. After what almost happened last night to your friend—"

"Jinx," Raven put in.

He nodded. "Anyway, after last night, I got to thinking. I know I can't stop all the predators out there, but with your help, I might be able to make some of them think twice about roaming around looking to grab kids like you."

"It's scary," Star whispered. "But we have to live and…"

"I know. I've been there. I get that."

The girls looked at him in shock. "You?" Raven said.

"A long time ago—but yeah. At the moment, though, that's not up for discussion. I need your input and maybe your help."

"Depends on what," Raven said, getting slight nods from Nickie and Star.

"Do you know any girls or guys who had something happen like what went down with Jinx last night?"

"There's been stories," Raven replied. "More like kids suddenly going missing—ones like us who work the streets. Yeah, some of them probably moved on. That happens. Try a new area, a new city. But others…" She spread her hands.

"I heard about one girl, who got into a car like Jinx did, and the guy drove off. She ain't been seen since," Nickie told him.

"I've been thinking," Raven said slowly. "Maybe we should tell the johns that if they want some, they get out and come into the alley with us. That's how some of the guys I know do it. They see a car that's cruising, they catch the dude looking at them then go into the alley. The dude parks and they take care of business where it's safe."

"Not really safe," Reaper told her. "But probably better than what I saw you doing tonight—and other kids like you."

"Hey, I tell the dude he turns off the car or I don't get in," Raven protested. "Taught them to do that too." She nodded at Nickie and Star.

"Did you tell that to Jinx?" Reaper asked.

"Well…yeah. Guess she forgot."

"He moved fast, just like any scumbag bent on grabbing one of you would. It only takes a second to pull you in, turn the car back on and take off before you know what has happened." Reaper shook his head before continuing. "What I need first from the three of you is to get the word out that I want to talk to any kids who managed to escape when someone tried to abduct them, and anyone who witnessed it."

"Reaper, ""right now like I told you, you're famous. I bet when we do that, you'll have girls flocking to you." Nickie grinned. "Tall, dark and handsome. Yeah, they'll want to meet you face-to-face."

"Good Lord." Reaper laughed. "Please tell me you didn't just say that."

"Well, you are," Nickie stated. "A little old maybe, but still…"

"Way to go, Nickie." Raven rolled her eyes before saying, "If we do find anyone who's interested, how can they hook up with you?"

Reaper tapped a finger to his lips. "You know the all-night diner on Prince Street?"

"Yeah. Frank's Place. Around the corner from Off-the-Street."

"That's the one. I'll show up there every night for the next week around four a.m. If I'm not there, tell them to give me a few minutes."

"'Cause you'll still be beating some asshole to a pulp," Raven said with a small grin.

"Now would I do that?" Reaper asked with a straight face.

"Yeah, you would. It's why you're famous," Nickie told him.

Reaper looked up at headlights approaching. The driver of the car slowed momentarily then sped up.

"You're killing our business," Raven muttered.

"Sorry, but…"

"Yeah, yeah, I know. This is more important. I get that. Okay, we'll see who we can dig up for you. What are you going to do if you get the info you want?"

"Go after the bastards," Reaper said tightly.

"I bet you catch them too." Star's smile was shy when she said that.

"For your sakes, I'm going to do all I can to make it happen."

* * * *

Reaper's plan was tenuous at best. The first step was to get leads from the kids about who the real predators were—presuming, of course, that they had it together enough that they remembered details.

Saying it was a guy in a green car and he looked around thirty isn't going to do me any good.

"And once I get the information," he murmured, as he got ready for bed, "then what? Make a list and pass it around to all the kids so they know who to watch out for? There's hundreds of them out there." He smiled dryly. "Tack flyers to every light pole saying, 'If you see anyone matching this description call 555-1234 ASAP'? Yeah, that'll work—not." That gave him an idea, though.

Chapter Three

"You are *what*?" Dallas looked at Zack as if he'd told him he was taking the next space shuttle to Mars.

"I'm going to stop bastards like the one who tried to grab Jinx last week."

It was Sunday. Almost noon. Dallas and Zack were finally getting dressed after spending what Dallas considered had been a very fruitful morning in bed.

"I'm going after them, once I get as much information as I can from the kids who witnessed — or were victims of — an attempted abduction."

Dallas glared at him. "Catching them is my business — police business. Don't you have any faith in us? After all, you're living with a cop. You know —"

"I know you do the best you can," Zack broke in. "Things would be a lot worse without all of you around. But" — he pointed a finger at Dallas — "you can't take things into your own hands the way I do. None of you can — at least, not legally."

Frustrated, but knowing Zack was correct, Dallas scrubbed one hand over his blond hair. "That's the only reason I condone what you do. I know what's out there, harassing the homeless, preying on kids. Add to that the problems the homeless have now, since our fucking city government set up the 'urban camping' ban."

Zack broke into a smile. "Such words from someone who is supposed to uphold the ban."

"Look, a lot of us don't like it, and you know it. But we have two choices, chase the homeless off, telling them to find a shelter or else, or look the other way. And if Off-the-Street is torn down to build those damned high-rises…" Dallas shook his head.

"You heard about that, huh?"

"Yeah. The people in the Uptown district are not happy. How did you know about it?"

"It's my business to be aware about things like that, so I can advise clients wanting to invest in new projects." Zack took a drink of his coffee. "Anyway, as I was saying, I'm going to get as much info as I can about the predators."

"Get it and turn it over to me. I'll pass it on."

"First off, how would you explain how you got it? And secondly, none of you can arrest any of the bastards unless you catch them in the act. You know the chances of that happening are slim to none."

Dallas' scowled in disgust. Not because of what Zack had pointed out, but because he knew his lover was correct. "And you can? Catch them, I mean?"

"If my plan works."

"Then what? You deal with them like you did with that one SOB?"

Zack nodded.

"What if they're an upstanding citizen of our fine city? They'll come after you, guns blazing."

"First off, even if they are, they still deserve what I'm going to do to them. Secondly, they have to find me first."

"You're not invisible, Zack."

Zack smiled dryly. "Maybe not, but I'm not 'me' either. I'm Reaper — the avenging shadow in the night. Damn, does that sound melodramatic or what?"

Dallas managed a laugh. "It does." He drummed a finger on the kitchen counter then picked up the cup of coffee he'd poured before Zack had dropped his bombshell. "Granted, the Reaper doesn't look like Zack Ward, investment counselor. But what if one of the predators is someone you've met at say...one of the charity events you attend?"

Zack snapped his fingers. "Speaking of which, and totally off the subject — "

"That you're trying to avoid right now," Dallas said, shaking his head.

"Not at all. But I have something else I want to deal with."

"Oh?"

"Yeah. I have to do what I can to find a new home for the shelter. I've done some research already and talked to a couple of my clients. Now I need to run it past Brian. Do you feel like taking a drive into town to the shelter?"

Dallas chuckled. "Beats taking our normal Sunday afternoon run."

With a grin, Zack patted Dallas' stomach. "Maybe we should do that first."

Dallas just flipped him off, saying, "Get your keys. You're driving."

* * * *

They went to Off-the-Street only to find out that Brian wasn't there, much to Zack's surprise.

"He's been taking the weekends off recently," one of the shelter's workers told Zack. "It's hard on him."

Zack nodded. He had the feeling he knew why, but he still needed to talk to Brian. So he called him, asking if he and Dallas could come by to visit. He chuckled when Brian told him bluntly that he expected to see them within the hour.

So now, they were standing on the porch of Brian's home, waiting for him to answer the doorbell.

It took a moment before the door opened to reveal a man in his early sixties, leaning heavily on a pair of forearm crutches.

"Come in. Come in," Brian said, moving to one side. "Haven't seen you in ages, Dallas. As for you, Zack…" Brian pulled him into a hug without losing control of the crutches. Stepping back, Brian looked Zack over. "You've lost a little weight."

"And you've gained some."

"Eh, maybe a couple of pounds. Unfortunately, I've had to use my wheelchair a lot more, now that I'm getting older. Sucks though, so when I can, I use these." He lifted one crutch. "But enough of my problems. Let's go into the living room and get comfortable."

Brian had lost most of the functionality in his lower limbs after a severe beating at the hands of some 'fucking SOBs', as he'd called them, who hadn't liked his stepping in to help a homeless man they were tormenting. Once he'd healed enough to be able to move around on crutches, he'd gone right back to Off-the-Street, the shelter that he'd started on a shoestring soon after getting out of the army in 1985.

That was where he and Zack had met ten years later, soon after Zack turned twenty. They had become friends with Brian, encouraging Zack to get off the streets and into school. It had taken time, but in the end,

Zack had gotten a job and his GED. Then he went to college—on a partial scholarship—coming out with a degree in finance with a minor in business administration. Five years later, he was licensed as a CFP and had started his own business.

"So, to what do I owe this honor?" Brian asked, once they were seated.

Zack and Dallas opted for the sofa, while Brian used his wheelchair.

"I can't just come for a visit?" Zack said.

"You can and do, but rarely. That says to me that you've got something on your mind."

"Caught me," Zack replied with a grin. Then he sobered. "I *know* you've heard about the tentative plans for the block housing the shelter."

"Yeah." Brian was obviously upset. "If the plans go through—and I'm afraid they will—I'm going to have to find a new building, and that is not going to be easy. Even if I can, how the hell will I pay for it?"

"That's why I'm here. You know that I have several well-to-do clients. One of them owns two properties that he's planning on selling, so that he can put the money to use in more profitable investments."

"And? It's not like I've got the money to buy one of them."

"First off, the one I'm think will work best for you is in the center of Uptown."

Dallas broke in, saying, "That's even worse than where the shelter is now."

"And closer to the people he's trying to help," Zack pointed out.

"True," Brian agreed. "That still doesn't help the financial problem."

"I talked to my client about that. He's willing to sell it for fifty-nine thousand and take the loss as a tax write-off."

Brian looked dismayed but still asked, "How big is the building?"

"Half again the size of what you have now. It's vacant and would need a lot of work to bring it up to code, according to him."

"More money I don't have." Brian shook his head. "Our donors are already beginning give less, because of the economy."

"Then we find new donors. That's the second part of my plan. With your permission and help, I want to have a fundraising gala." Zack smiled, adding, "One that people will be talking about for years to come."

"You can do that?"

"Brian, when I set my mind to it, I can do just about anything. I have contacts through my clients — people with too much disposable income. Like the man who owns the building I told you about, they're looking for tax write-offs, and donations are one way to get them."

"How would we go about this? Presuming I think the building will work?"

For the next hour, they discussed options. Zack got on Brian's computer to show him the building in question then promised to take him to see it in person once he got the keys from his client. Dallas said he knew the building, since it was in his district, and although the neighborhood was bad, that particular street was better than some. "The usual 'stay off of that one if you don't want to be mugged, but it's safe to be on this one before dark'," he explained.

By the time they finished talking, Brian seemed more hopeful that there would be a new home for the shelter.

"Hell," Brian said, "maybe it's time to move anyway. A bigger place, closer to the people who need it. Yeah. I like." He looked at Zack hopefully. "*If* we can pull it off."

"We will. I promise. Now Dallas and I have something else we need to do before it gets dark."

Dallas groaned. "Run."

"Yep." Zack grinned evilly. "Brian, I'll be in contact as soon as I get permission for us to visit the building. Hopefully that will be within the next couple of days. Will you be at the shelter?"

"Always am. Well, during the week. Damn it, I hate getting old. Used to be even with those." Brian pointed to the crutches. "I was able to run the place twenty-four-seven. Now..." He sighed.

"You still do twice what most of the people you've got working there do. You deserve to take the weekends off. So quit your bitching," Zack said, gripping his shoulder.

"Yeah, yeah." Brian covered Zack's hand with his own. "Thank you for that and for everything you're doing for me and for the kids."

"I owe you a debt I can never repay," Zack replied softly.

"Bull. You'd have made it off the streets without me."

"But you gave me the drive to do more than just... Well, you know."

"Yeah, I know. Now will you get out of here before we both get maudlin? And show the kid"—Brian grinned at Dallas—"you've still got what it takes by running circles around him."

"Sure going to try."

* * * *

"Beat you," Dallas crowed, reaching the bedroom before Zack did.

"Only because you're a youngster," Zack protested.

"Thirty-two is not a youngster. And you're hardly in your dotage yet."

"I'm nine years—"

"Don't," Dallas said. "Don't *even* go there. You're in your prime and I like you that way. As a matter of fact, I'm going to prove I do while we shower."

"Are you now?"

"Yeah. So get moving."

Dallas laughed when Zack saluted before beginning to strip out of his running gear.

'As soon as both men were standing in the shower, the hot water beating down on them, Dallas soaped up a washcloth. Slowly, he began washing his lover, paying special attention to Zack's nipples before working his way down, following the fine line of dark hair that led to Zack's groin and now-hardening cock. Zack groaned when Dallas clearly ignored his cock and balls, moving on to his legs and feet before having him turn around so he could do his back.

Finished, Dallas stood, smiling wickedly as he handed the washcloth to Zack.

"And what am I supposed to do with this?" Zack teased.

"Use it on me."

With a grin, Zack rolled it up, employing it to swat Dallas' ass.

"Not like that, you nut," Dallas grumbled.

"Like this, then?" Zack asked. He soaped the cloth and set to work. Unlike Dallas, Zack spent time making certain—after he'd finished washing the rest of Dallas—that every inch of his lover's throbbing cock had been attended to.

"Are you trying to make me come before I get a chance to screw you?" Dallas asked with a laugh, moving under the shower to rinse off.

"Umm... That would be no," Zack replied. He rinsed off as well, before turning to face the shower wall, placing his hands against it.

Dallas took the lube from the shelf, oiled two fingers and pushed one through Zack's tight hole to find and stroke his gland. "Like that, do you?" he murmured when Zack moaned deeply.

"You know damned well I do," Zack muttered. "But I want more. I want your dick in me—the sooner the better."

After using both fingers to stretch Zack, Dallas pulled them out and placed the bulbous head of his cock against Zack's entrance. He thrust in, stopping to allow Zack to get used to him. Then, carefully, he went deeper until Zack's tight channel engulfed Dallas' cock.

"Ready?" Dallas asked. With one hand on Zack's hip, he gripped his lover's throbbing member with his other hand.

"I was ready an hour ago," Zack informed him, eliciting a low chuckle from Dallas in reply.

Then Dallas began to ride him—slowly at first. Soon they were moving together with practiced ease, their emotions riding high with the pleasure they were giving each other. Dallas came first, exploding with a shout that echoed off the shower walls. Zack's cry of release came moments later, the tightening of his channel when he did milking the last of Dallas' cum from his still semi-rigid cock.

"Not sure," Dallas managed to get out between pants.

"What?" Zack said, his breathing finally normalizing.

"Not sure I have the energy to move." He leaned against Zack, pressing him to the shower wall. "So we may be here a while."

Zack snorted. "You say that every time we do it this way."

"True, but…" Putting his hands against the wall, Dallas then pulled out and moved away. When Zack turned to wrap him in a tight embrace, they fell back against the wall, kissing deeply.

"Now I really don't want to move," Dallas murmured.

Zack reached over to train the shower on him.

"Goddamn it!"

"Now will you?" Zack asked, turning off the ice-cold water.

Dallas did, grumbling about sadistic lovers as they got out and toweled dry. Dallas wrapped a towel around his waist, muttering, "We could go down in the nude to fix supper.

Zack laughed. "We could, but we won't. Spattering hot grease—"

"Yeah, yeah. I know."

After giving Zack a quick hug, they got dressed and headed down to the kitchen.

Chapter Four

"I need every detail you can remember," Reaper said, glancing from one teen to the next. "No matter how small."

As he'd hoped, Raven and the other girls had gotten the word out, and over the past three nights, he'd met several teens at the diner, Frank's Place—girls and guys, who had either witnessed an attempted abduction or had been the intended victim. Some he had eliminated as their information was sketchy at best. The others, eight of them, had agreed to meet with him again to compare notes. Now it was going on three a.m. on Thursday morning, and they were gathered in the back room of the diner, away from prying eyes.

"First, describe the cars," Reaper said.

"The one I saw," a slender eighteen-year-old who called himself Zip said, "was a Chevy. A Malibu, I'm pretty sure. About four years old. Sort of brown with a gray interior."

"Yeah, I saw that one too. It's missing a hubcap," one of the girls said.

"The one I saw was dark red. A Ford. I know it was new. This year or last. Nothing to make it stand out other than the color," a kid named Scooby told Zack.

China raised her hand. "Black Honda here." She shivered. "Dude driving it was old, like maybe forty. He had slicked back blond hair and wore wrap-around sunglasses, even though it was night. He was dressed kinda geeky in one of those stupid V-neck, button-down sweaters. And he's not too strong—or I wouldn't be here now."

"Fuck, that's the same dude I saw trying to grab Cassie, I bet," another girl said.

"The guy I saw was big. Like he works out," Pinky told them. "His car might have been the same brown one you saw, Zip. I was more interested in the guy. He was kinda cute, if you like red-haired older men with mustaches."

Reaper listened, taking notes. He thought he remembered the red car. If it was the same one, it had driven around through the neighborhood where he'd stopped Jinx's kidnapping—several times, in fact. Usually after the bars had closed. But then a lot of the same cars did that as the bar patrons headed home for the night.

Finally Reaper said, "All right, we have three different cars and two men driving them, so far."

"Three," Scooby told him. "The guy in the red car was thirty or so. Curly black hair, real tan."

"Hispanic?" Reaper asked him.

"Could be. I know he was wearing a lot of bling because it caught the light when he was talking to the guy he tried to grab. Damn, that kid couldn't have been more that fourteen. What is the world coming to?"

Reaper repressed a smile. Scooby was, best guess, barely sixteen.

China raised her hand again. "I was talking to some of the other girls I run with. Two of them said they got real bad vibes from a dude in a Camaro. Big, fat slob. He wanted them to do him in a parking lot behind a building. I tried to get them to come talk to you but they weren't having any of that. One of them said he has a bad comb-over." She chuckled. "She said the brown hair on his pasty white skull made him look like the guy who was mayor of New York. Not that I know who that is, but..." She shrugged.

"I know who she means," Reaper told her. "The mayor wasn't fat, but the description of the hair could help. Is there anything else any of you can think of?"

The teens all shook their heads.

"Will any of this help you?" Zip asked.

Suddenly Scooby slapped his hand on the table. "License plate for the Ford. I didn't get the whole thing but I think the first two digits were A4. Of course it could have been AA, but I'm real sure the first one was an A."

"Great. So we have a start. Now on to the next bit of business. Since you guys have the best idea of what these men look like, as well as their cars, I want you to call me if you spot them again."

"I don't have a phone," Pinky said.

Reaper opened the bag he'd set on the floor beside him, taking out eight throwaway phones then handed them out. "Now you do," he told her. "All of you use these. They're GPS modified so when you call, I'll know right where you are." He gave them his number, telling them to put it on speed dial. "And get the word out about these guys to everyone you know. They're probably not the only predators running around, but my stopping them is a start."

"You know they ain't," Zip said. "But yeah, if you take care of them, we'll all feel a bit safer."

"That's the plan," Reaper replied before dismissing them.

Now I have to keep my eyes open, and if one of them calls, hope I'm close enough to get to them before something bad goes down.

* * * *

"What information did you get from the kids?" Dallas asked the moment he got home around eight in the morning and joined Zack in the bedroom. "I'm not going to turn it in, because you were right. There's no way I could explain how I got it. But I want to know who to watch out for."

After running the comb through his hair one more time to tame it for work, Zack turned from the mirror to look at him, one eyebrow arched. "No good morning? No kiss?"

"Good morning." Dallas stepped close enough to give him his kiss and muss his hair, earning a growl of frustration from his lover. "Now, what did you learn?" he asked, sitting on the bed to take off his shoes.

Zack laid it out in detail, ending by saying, "It's not much, I know, but more than I had before."

"*We* had," Dallas emphasized.

"We had. I know I've seen that red Ford a few times soon after the bars have closed for the night. Well, if it's the same one. Next time I see it, I'll check the license plate. If Scooby's right, it's AA or A4 something."

"Not enough for me to run, unfortunately." Dallas unbuttoned his shirt and gave it to Zack when he held out his hand.

"Want me to drop those" — Zack pointed to the small pile of uniforms on the chair — "off at the cleaners?"

"I'd love you forever if you did."

"That's what it takes?" Zack asked, grinning.

"Well...that and good sex, companionship and decent meals and — "

Zack stopped him with a kiss. "I think we have all of that. But most of all, real love."

"We do," Dallas agreed, pulling him down for another kiss. "Now off with you or you'll be late. Especially" — he grinned — "since you have a stop to make on the way in."

Zack paused long enough to re-comb his hair before picking up the uniforms to take with him. On his way past Dallas, he bent to give him one final kiss then left.

* * * *

"Brian, can you be free in an hour?" Zack asked when he got his mentor on the phone just after four on Thursday afternoon.

Brian said he could be, asking if they were going to go look at the building. Zack told him they were and that he'd pick him up in front of the shelter.

Almost exactly an hour later, Zack got out of the car and opened the passenger door for Brian. He took Brian's crutches when he handed them over, stowing them in the back seat.

Tyler, the street where the building was located, held a mixture of older, dilapidated apartment buildings and rooming houses, as well as two bars, a small family-owned grocery store, a thrift shop and a liquor store. Teens and older people were walking down the street, sitting on stoops, or lolling against the walls of the various establishments.

"Not exactly Shangri La," Brian commented once they were parked and standing on the sidewalk. "Be sure to lock the car."

"Of course." Zack had shed his suit coat and tie then rolled up his sleeves so, while he didn't exactly fit into the neighborhood, he didn't stand out either. Brian, as was his wont, wore an older pair of jeans and a sweatshirt.

After taking out the keys his client had given him, Zack opened the front door of the derelict building that, he hoped, would meet with Brian's approval as a new home for the shelter.

The place had been a print shop in its last life. The front room was large with a counter cutting it in half. What was left of the counter now stood—or lay—in pieces in the front of the room. Wallpaper hung in tatters on one wall, obviously the victim of water damage. Two doors at the back of the room opened onto equally large rooms that ran the depth of the rest of the building. They were now empty except for a few heavy, broken tables. Stairs along the back wall of the front room led to the second floor with another set behind a locked door, going down to a basement.

"Do you think you can make it up?" Zack asked bluntly. He took in the fact the stair railing was almost non-existent and two of the steps were only partially there.

"For damned sure going to try," Brian replied, carefully setting his crutches on the bottom stair.

Cautiously, testing each step first, he worked his way to the second floor with Zack right behind him to catch him if something went wrong. When he got to the top, Brian let out a deep breath.

"That was *not* fun." He chuckled dryly. "And I have to go back down them, sooner or later."

"I'll toss you over my shoulder and carry you down," Zack said with a grin as he opened the first door off the hallway where they now stood. "Seems like someone partied hard up here."

Beer cans and beer and whiskey bottles lay strewn around the room, along with fast-food wrappers and, Zack noted, some syringes. The room behind it was equally as messy, while a third one at the back of the building held a few rotting blankets and sleeping bags. Across from them, along the hallway that traversed the building from front to back, were five more smaller rooms that had also, from the look of them, been sleeping areas for homeless kids—or adults.

"Used to be someone's squat, I'd say," Brian commented. "Wonder why they moved out?"

Zack pointed to some faded gang tags on the walls. "Competition."

"It's been a while, though, since anyone's been up here, if the dust and dirt are any indication."

"Yes. My client hired a security company to keep an eye on the place once he realized what was going on," Zack told him

"Too bad he didn't hire a cleaning company too," Brian muttered. "How the hell did he plan on selling it the way it is?"

"That, according to him, is why he's willing to let you have it so cheap. He figures it's less expensive than his doing anything to the building."

"How pragmatic of him." Brian pounded his fist on one wall. "Sturdy."

"Yep. Physically the building is all right. Well, if you don't count the stairs. There was an elevator but the city red-tagged it, he said."

"Where?"

They went into the hallway again, and Zack pointed to the end where there was an open shaft with a gate across the front.

"I'll have to do something about that, for sure," Brian commented.

"So you're considering it?"

"Probably." Brian sighed when they got back to where they'd started, looking at the stairs going up to the third floor. They were in no better condition than the ones leading down. "Not sure I'm ready to tackle those."

"Stay here. I'll check it out."

Zack found the third floor was in much the same condition as the second, although there was less detritus and more dirt and dust. He noted a trap door leading up to the roof with a new padlock on the hasp to keep it locked. As with the lower floor, there was a hallway with several small rooms off each side of it and one larger one by the stairs.

"I wonder," Zack said when he rejoined Brian and described the third floor, "if this was a hotel way back when? Or maybe a rooming house, since there's only a couple of bathrooms on each floor."

"Wouldn't surprise me," Brian replied as he began easing his way down to the ground floor. Once they were back in the front room, Brian leaned against a part of the counter that was still standing. "It definitely has potential, but it's going to cost a small fortune to fix up."

Zack nodded. "It won't be cheap, but it's not like you're starting from scratch. You have all the furniture from where you are now, and the kitchen appliances. And you have a built-in work crew once the city deems the building up to code."

"True enough. Knowing the kids who are regulars, a lot of them will be willing to help out."

"Yep. Let me check out the basement."

The basement was, much to Zack's surprise, relatively clean. Probably, he figured, because it had been locked off and there were no windows. At the moment, all it held was the building's heating system and a padlocked box on one wall for, according to the sign on the front, the electrical breakers.

Going back to where Brian waited, Zack told him what he'd found before saying, "Let's get you back to the shelter. I'll call my client in the morning to tell him you're interested and give him your number. Then I'll start the ball rolling on the gala to raise the money you'll need."

"Thank you! Thank you for...everything you're doing."

"Hey, no thanks needed. Without you, I wouldn't be in a position to do anything other than be a member of the work crew once they get started."

"No, Zack," Brian said as he started toward the front door. "You'd have gotten off the streets, even without my help. I just gave you a push in the right direction."

"More like a hard shove," Zack retorted with a grin. "Still..."

"Enough!" Brian stopped when they got outside, looking up and down the now darkening street. "Yeah, not the best area in the city, but one that needs the shelter."

Two teens, who were walking toward them, stopped momentarily then hurried forward. "Mr. Foster," one boy said, "What are you doing around here? It's not...well...safe, you know."

"Yeah, Pike, I know," Brian replied with a smile. "But if things go the way I'm hoping, it will be safer. At least inside there." He nodded toward the building. When Pike asked why, Brian told him what might happen.

"Woot," Micky, the other boy, said, pumping his fist in the air. "If you need grunt work…"

"I'll let you know," Brian told him with a smile. "Trust me on that one."

"Mr. Foster," Pick said seriously. "We all trust you. Honest. You're good people." Then, looking embarrassed that he'd been so open, Zack supposed, Pike walked away quickly with Micky right behind him.

"That right there," Brian said as he got into the car, "is what makes all this worth it."

Chapter Five

Reaper moved swiftly but silently down the dark alley. It had been a long night and he was both frustrated and tired. Frustrated because he hadn't seen any of the cars or the men who might be involved in the attempted abductions of the street kids he considered his charges. Tired because he'd gotten home much later than he usually did, thanks to showing Brian the building that they both hoped would become the new Off-the-Street shelter. Normally, he would get home, eat then sleep for six hours before beginning his rounds of the streets. Tonight, he'd gotten four hours and was feeling it.

The reason he was being so quiet at the moment had to do with the muffled sobs he'd heard seconds earlier when passing the alley. He knew it could be a kid having a nightmare as they slept in a doorway or under a loading dock. But it also could mean the kid was in trouble.

"Hold still, faggot," a male said.

His words were followed by a muffled titter from what Reaper presumed was a second person.

Reaper rounded a tall dumpster to find two men, one in his late teens, the other a few years older. The older, bulkier one had a blond-haired kid shoved face first against the dirty brick wall of the alley. The victim was struggling, but to no avail, as the guy holding him there pulled down the 'kid's' ragged jeans.

"You know you want this," the guy said. "All you faggots do."

"Please…" the boy whimpered.

"See, told you he did," the assailant said to his companion.

"Having a party, punks?" Reaper asked menacingly.

The assailant glanced quickly over his shoulder. "Yeah, and you ain't invited."

"I beg to differ." Reaper stepped in, wrapping his arm around the guy's throat in a choke hold to pull him away from his victim.

Suddenly, unexpectedly, the teen who had been watching plunged a knife into Reaper's shoulder, shouting, "Let him go, you fucker. He's only doing what the fag wanted him to."

Ignoring the searing pain, Reaper tightened his hold on the punk's throat. "Back off, you snot-nosed brat, or you friend here will end up… Well, dead." Reaper turned sharply as he said that, avoiding getting stabbed a second time. Instead, the blade the teen was using jabbed into the larger guy's side. With his free hand, Reaper managed to grab the teen's wrist before he could pull out of reach. Reaper twisted hard, and the teen let out a cry of pain, dropping the knife.

"Where's a damned cop when you need one," Reaper muttered as he loosened his hold on the potential rapist. He didn't let him go, however. He just didn't want him dying.

Well, I'd like him dead, but that's not what I do.

"You…" Reaper glared as the teen, who was holding his injured wrist against his chest. "Down on the ground, on your stomach — now."

"Fuck you!"

Reaper smiled grimly. "Do it, or your friend here gets hurt worse than he is already." Reaper tightened his hold again at the same time that he reached around to grab his prisoner's balls, squeezing hard.

"He ain't no friend," the teen said. He turned and sprinted toward the end of the alley. Seconds later, he vanished from sight.

Still holding his prisoner, Reaper finally looked at the kid who has been the target of the assault. The boy had sunk down to the pavement, his back against the wall, his arms wrapped tightly around his knees.

"Are you…? Never mind, that would have been a stupid question," Reaper said gruffly. "As for you…" He returned his attention to the attacker, forcing him down to his knees. "I'm debating between beating you to a pulp and calling the cops. Got any druthers on which I do?"

"Fuck you!"

"Are those the only two words you and your friend know?"

"Fuck—" The punk's words were cut off when Reaper punched him hard in the mouth.

"You're bleeding," the blond boy said, looking up at Reaper.

"Flesh wound," Reaper replied, although now that it had been pointed out to him, he had the feeling it was a bit worse than that. Gritting his teeth, he punched the punk again, knocking him flat on his back and out cold.

The boy stood slowly, pulling up his jeans. "Thank you," he whispered. "Oh…God…" Tears started streaming down his face.

"You want to thank me? Find something I can use to tie up this piece of trash."

The kid nodded, wiping away the tears. He scuttled down the alley, returning a minute later with a garbage-covered length of rope. Reaper used it to bind the attacker's hands behind his back after rolling him none too gently onto his face. Then, wincing in pain, he hauled the punk up high enough to tip him into the dumpster.

"Wonder if anyone will find him before the trash truck comes by to pick up the garbage."

"I hope not," the teen spat angrily.

"Let's get out of here," Reaper said.

The blond grabbed his fallen backpack and dug through it as they walked out of the alley. "Hold still," he said, when he found what he'd been searching for. Standing on tiptoe, he pressed something against Reaper's shoulder where the knife had gone in. Then, much to Reaper's surprise, he wrapped a belt around it and under Reaper's arm, pulling it tight. Fire shot through Reaper's shoulder for a moment then eased back to a slow burn.

"Where'd you learn how to do that?" Reaper asked him.

"You live the way I do, you learn," he replied sadly.

"Yeah. True. Okay. You got somewhere to stay?"

When the kid shook his head, Reaper told him to follow him. "What's your name?" Reaper asked while they walked the three blocks to his car.

"Umm…Mango?"

Reaper chuckled. "Okay, Mango. I'm going to take you to a shelter. I expect you to stay there long enough to get some real sleep and eat. Understand?"

"Yes…" Mango hesitated. "You're Reaper, aren't you?"

"Yep." Reaper unlocked the car, waited for Mango to get in, then he got in too. As he drove to Off-the-Street, he told Mango, "You should get yourself a weapon of some sort."

"Got one," Mango said shyly, showing him the knife the smaller punk had used to stab Reaper.

"That works. Just remember to use it if it comes down to it.

"Yes, sir."

Reaper pulled up in front of the shelter, nodded when Mango thanked him again then watched to make certain the kid went inside before driving off, heading home.

* * * *

"Zack's been hurt," Mrs. Cook said the moment Dallas walked into the kitchen. "Said someone tried to mug him. I found him in the living room when I came in, bloody and—"

The rest of her words were lost as Dallas raced upstairs to the bedroom.

Zack was seated on the edge of the bed, one arm in the sleeve of the shirt he was trying to put on. He looked pale and drawn, but determined.

"What the hell do you think you're doing?" Dallas asked tightly as he approached Zack.

"Getting ready to go into work," Zack replied, not looking at him.

"Like hell." Dallas dropped to his knees in front of Zack.

"Now is not the time," Zack muttered through pinched lips, obviously trying to smile—unsuccessfully.

"You're right." Dallas gently took hold of the shirt and removed it. "Let me see," he said, looking at Zack's bandaged shoulder.

"Nothing much to see. It's just a minor stab wound." Zack sighed, complying when Dallas told him to lie back. "Mrs. Cook took care of it."

Dallas sat beside him, carefully pulling back the tape that held the thick wad of gauze in place. "Minor, my ass," he muttered, even though he could see the knife had only penetrated flesh. But the cut was a nasty one. He suspected the blade had hit bone and slid off and up. "Why the hell didn't you go to the ER?"

"And tell them what?"

"The same thing you told Mrs. Cook. That someone tried to mug you."

"Then the cops would have been called and…" Zack spread his hands.

"What happened? Exactly."

Zack told him. Dallas' frown deepened as he listened until the end. Then he smiled — barely.

"You have a thing for punks and dumpsters all of a sudden."

Zack shrugged his uninjured shoulder. "Whatever works."

"Why didn't you call me for backup?"

"I was sort of busy dealing with those two sons of bitches and keeping the kid safe. Besides, how would you have explained it to Mike?"

"I'd have thought of something." Dallas carefully re-taped the gauze, asking, "Did she at least put some antibiotic cream on it?"

"Yeah, after she scrubbed it. That woman is heartless," Zack muttered.

"Better than you getting an infection."

"Mind if I get dressed now?"

"Yeah, I do. I think you can miss one day of work. In fact, mister, you're going to stay in bed until this time tomorrow, and do *not* argue with me," Dallas said pointedly when it appeared as if Zack was going to.

"It's only a damned flesh wound. I've had a lot worse done to me in my life."

"Back when you were young and able to handle it."

"Right. Play the age card."

"I will, if that's what it takes," Dallas told him. "I'm going to shower, and if you're not here when I get back, your ass is in big trouble."

"From you, it's not trouble. It's—"

"Not what you're getting until you heal." Dallas waggled his eyebrows. "Does that give you a reason to rest and get better?"

"It does," Zack admitted, closing his eyes. He smiled when Dallas leaned over to kiss his forehead. He started to say something, and seconds later, was asleep.

You are too much, my man. Too impetuous, too daring, too…too caring. And those are only a few of the reasons why I love you.

Chapter Six

Zack did adhere to Dallas' wishes and had spent twenty-four hours either in bed or on the computer putting together his plans for the fundraising gala for Off-the-Street. He'd awakened late in the afternoon when Dallas had and they'd cuddled for a while, but that was all. Between the ache in his shoulder and the doses of aspirin Dallas had foisted on him, Zack had the feeling he couldn't have performed no matter how badly he might have wanted to.

The following morning, however, Zack was up, dressed and down in the kitchen, about to dig into a hearty breakfast of pancakes and sausage when Dallas came home from work.

"Thank God," Zack whispered, after making certain Mrs. Cook wasn't within earshot. "She's been mothering me like I was going to die any second now."

Dallas snorted in amusement. "And you love it."

"Okay, it *is* nice—I guess. Never got that from..." Zack snapped his mouth shut, not wanting to rehash his past.

"I know," Dallas replied compassionately, giving him a gentle hug. "And it still hurts after all these years."

"Almost thirty years. You wouldn't think it would but... Well, I guess that's life." Quickly changing the subject, Zack asked Dallas, "So how did your night go?"

"Other than the normal traffic stops? We caught three kids trying to break into a clothing store. Broke up a fight between a couple of gang members and a potential one between two very drunk men outside of Tommy's Bar."

"And survived in one piece."

"Don't I always?"

"No." Zack remembered a time eight years ago when he'd spent two days at the hospital watching over Dallas while his lover recuperated from a gunshot wound.

"All right. Most of the time." Dallas saluted Mrs. Cook when she returned to the kitchen, smiling when she told him to sit and eat.

"It's not often I see both of you in the morning at the same time," she lamented. "Usually you grab something on your way out," she said pointedly to Zack. "And you..." She shook a finger at Dallas.

"Come on," Dallas said. "I sit and eat. Well, half the time anyway." He grinned. "It's hard to make a sandwich out of pancakes or French toast."

"Not that you haven't tried. Well, now that you're here—and he's here too—I expect you both to eat everything in front of you."

"Yes, Mama," Dallas replied, hugging her before he sat.

She set his plate in front of him, poured him juice then put her hand on Zack's forehead. "No temperature, but really, Zack. Don't you think you should stay in bed for another day? It *is* Saturday."

"I have to go talk to Brian about the gala then do another walk-through of the building he's going to buy — or we hope he's going to. I want to make certain I didn't miss anything vital Thursday afternoon."

"Want me to come with you?" Dallas asked.

"You need to sleep."

"It's eight-thirty. I'll be in bed by nine. Hold off until three then wake me up. That'll give me time before my shift starts."

"You need more sleep than —"

"Don't fuss over me," Dallas grumbled. "If you can survive on six hours of sleep, so can I."

"We'll compromise. I'll wake you at four."

"Deal."

* * * *

Zack and Brian spent an hour at Brian's house going over the plans for the gala.

Brian was doubtful, as he had been since the beginning, that Zack could pull it off. "I mean the Gold Hotel? Come on. They'll charge more than we'll make in donations."

"Not when one of my clients is both on their board and behind this one hundred percent."

"You and your clients." Brian shook his head. "Is there any bigwig in the city you don't know and work for?"

Zack laughed. "Tons. It's just luck that I happen to work with some who can — and are willing — to help with this."

When they were finished, Brian asked if Zack had plans for the day.

"Other than taking Dallas to see the building late this afternoon? Not a one. Why?"

"Feel like keeping my company while I go dog hunting?"

Zack cocked an eyebrow. "You're getting a dog?"

"I know. Crazy, huh? But I figure I could use the companionship on the weekends." Brian smiled wryly. "I thought I'd like having time to myself away from the shelter and all the noise and action and what have you. And I did, for a while."

"I totally get that. Sure, I'll come along. Your car or mine?"

"Mine," Brian said firmly. His car was equipped with hand controls for braking and accelerating, giving him the freedom he needed to drive to and from the shelter and run errands. "God help me when I'm confined to the wheelchair," he said when they got into the car. "Then I suppose I'll have to get one of those vans that are wheelchair accessible."

"Twenty years from now," Zack replied, patting his shoulder.

"Your words to God's ear."

When they arrived at the animal shelter—which was busy, being Saturday—one of the attendants asked Brian what kind of dog he was looking for.

"A calm one, for starters—and big. Well, not Mastiff big but not some whiny poodle either."

"I have the perfect dog for you," she said, eyeing his crutches. "Kozak."

"Weird name," Brian commented as he and Zack followed her into the dog room.

Halfway down an aisle of cages, she stopped. When Brian looked into the cage, he lifted his eyebrows in surprise. "That's a greyhound. Don't they...? They race. I don't think..."

The woman laughed. "That's a common misconception. Greyhounds are the ultimate couch potatoes. Especially Kozak." When she said his name, the coal-black greyhound stood and came to the door, revealing as he did that he was missing his right hind leg.

Brian looked at the dog then at the attendant. "You figure we'd be well matched because we're both handicapped?" he asked sardonically.

"Well" — she smiled — "that did occur to me."

"What the hell. Can you let him out?"

She did, and Brian reached down to pet Kozak. The dog leaned in to Brian's touch, gazing up at him with what seemed to Zack to be a pleading look.

"How long has he been here?" Brian asked.

"Too long," the woman replied with some asperity. "Thankfully, we're a no-kill shelter."

"How hard would he be to take care of?"

She explained the dog's needs, agreeing with Brian that his having a large backyard would be a plus under the circumstances. "You should walk Kozak, when you can, but letting him run and play in the yard will do just as well."

"Would you like to come home with me?" Brian asked Kozak. The dog licked his hand, as if replying in the affirmative. "Then it's a done deal."

Once the papers were signed and the adoption fee paid, Brian bought a collar and leash for Kozak, as well as pet bowls and food, all of which the shelter had for sale. Some of the workers came out to say goodbye to the dog, one of them bringing the toys he'd had in his cage. Then Brian led Kozak out to the car with Zack trailing behind with all the purchases.

Kozak easily and eagerly, leaped into the back seat. As soon as Brian was seated, the dog nuzzled the side of his neck.

Zack watched, grinning, before putting everything in the trunk of the car and joining them. "I think you have a friend for life."

"Well, that's the idea, isn't it?" Brian said, reaching back to pat Kozak's head before putting the car in gear and pulling out of the lot.

* * * *

Zack sat beside Dallas, studying him as he slept. "I still wonder," he said softly, "how I got so lucky to find you?"

Dallas looked up at him, rubbing his eyes. "I was the lucky one."

"We both were, I think," Zack replied, kissing him. "Now, up and at 'em. We have places to go and things to do."

"Don't wanna," Dallas grumbled. "Can I just do you before going to work?"

"A tempting offer, but no." Zack took Dallas' hands and pulled him upright. "Now you put your feet on the floor, stand, and…"

"Got it." Dallas freed one hand, cupped the nape of Zack's neck and kissed him. "Sure we can't stay here?" He patted the bed.

With a definite eye roll, Zack got up. "Go." He pointed to the bathroom.

Muttering that Zack was no fun, Dallas did. Several minutes later, he was dressed, with his uniform in his bag. "Because I don't think my going to look at the building dressed for work would be the brightest idea I've ever had."

Zack agreed. He was wearing the same dark jeans and black long-sleeved T-shirt he'd had on when he'd gone to see Brian. "Casual works."

* * * *

When they arrived at the building, Zack found a parking spot in the small lot behind it. He locked the car, set the alarm and entered the building through the back door. The moment they were inside, Dallas put a finger to his lips. Zack realized why a moment later as he heard sounds of movement from the second floor.

"Someone crashing?" Dallas murmured.

"Best guess, yes. But let's not take any chances," Zack barely whispered. "There were gang tags on the walls up there, though they were old ones."

Dallas didn't seem the least bit surprised when Zack took his knife from its waistband sheath, holding it in one hand as they made their way to the stairs.

Zack pointed to himself then the stairs, indicating Dallas should hang back for the moment. Dallas nodded, and Zack began his slow ascent, trying to avoid the worst of the steps to keep them from creaking. When he got to the top, he paused to locate the intruders. Soft voices came from the room at the back. Zack made his way there then inched the door open.

Three teens — two male and one female — sat huddled together, sharing a joint. Zack recognized one of them and stepped into the room after shaking his head to make his hair fall the way Reaper wore it.

Should have worn my leathers. Oh, well. At least my shirt passes, more or less.

He also sheathed the knife, but kept his hand on the hilt for the moment.

"Hell," the younger teen groaned, trying to hide the joint behind his back.

"Not working, Taxi," Zack told him. He eyed the others, grinning slightly. "Smoke 'em if you got 'em, as they used to say in the Army, way back when."

"You know this dude?" the older boy asked Taxi.

"Yeah. It's Reaper. What are you doing here, man? Thought you only came out at night," Taxi said somewhat defiantly.

"I'm always around," Zack told him.

"Keeping us safe," the girl said. "Least that's the story."

"It's the truth," Zack agreed. He stiffened, aware someone was behind him from the looks on the teens' faces and hoped to hell it was Dallas.

"Shit, I know that guy. He's a cop," the older boy exclaimed. "Reaper, get out!" He pointed to a half-open window.

Zack turned to look. "Well, hello, Officer Comstock. To what do we owe this pleasure?"

"Saw the front door open and decided to check things out," Dallas replied without missing a beat. He looked at the kids. "Tank, good thing marijuana's legal now or I'd have to arrest you, even though I'm not in uniform."

"Yeah, you're outta luck, this time," Tank muttered.

Dallas smiled. "I'm sure I'll have other chances. You three might want to vacate the premises, though. You *are* trespassing."

"Yes, sir," the girl said, jumping to her feet.

"You" — Dallas shot a hard look at Zack — "I want to have a few words with."

The kids eased their way toward the window and moments later, they were through it. Zack heard the rattle of their footsteps as they raced down the fire escape.

"Well, *Reaper*, what now?" Dallas asked with a grin. "Do I bring you in?"

Zack snorted. "If you were going to do that, you'd have done it years ago. Now we do what we came for — check out the building. And hope we don't find anyone else using it."

Chapter Seven

It was well after two a.m. Tuesday morning when Reaper spotted one of the cars he was looking for by its color and the license plate. It was AA, not A4, as Scooby had said, and it was a newer Fiesta. From the driver's silhouette, he had curly hair. Reaper was too far away to tell if it was black or not, but he was dead certain it was his man.

The car was moving slowly down the street. Two blocks ahead of it, Reaper could see a couple of girls standing by the proverbial streetlight. Keeping deep in the shadow of the buildings, Reaper raced after the car. As he did, he felt his phone vibrate at his waist. Stopping only long enough to read the short message, he texted back *I'm here*, knowing at that point one of the girls he saw had been at the meeting at Frank's Place.

The car slowed even more, inching over to the curb in front of the girls. Whatever the driver said made the taller girl wave her hand in negation and back away. The shorter one, however, stepped up to the car, crouching to talk to the driver. She gestured toward an alley half a block away. Zack could see the driver shake his head then, seconds later, nod.

The car crept forward, stopping right in front of the alley, while the girl hurried down the street and stopped just inside the entrance. The driver got out, leaving the car door open, and walked toward his prey. By then, Reaper was directly across the street from them. He heard a muffled cry as the driver grabbed the girl and saw him cover the girl's mouth with his hand while wrapping his arm around her waist. She struggled when he started back to the car.

Reaper moved to the car. He closed the door and was pressed against the wall next to the alley when the man finally carried the girl out to the dark sidewalk. Now that he had a clear view of her, Reaper recognized the girl. It was China, the one who had always raised her hand at the meeting before speaking. She continued to struggle, raking her nails up the man's arm. It didn't help her gain her freedom, but it did keep the man's attention focused on her long enough for Reaper grab a handful of his hair and yank his head back.

The abductor let out a shout of surprise, mixed with a bit of pain. His hold loosened on China as he moved his hand from her mouth to his waistband, but he didn't let her go. When he raised his hand again, he was holding a knife.

"Bet mine's bigger than yours," Reaper said, pushing the point of the blade just under the man's ear.

The man's reply was to shove China away hard enough that she landed on her hands and knees on the pavement. Then he jerked his head forward, spun around and thrust his knife toward Reaper's gut. Only Reaper wasn't standing where his assailant had expected, as the man found out seconds later when Reaper's boot landed hard and fast on his hip. The man staggered then regained his footing, but it was too late. Reaper slammed him against the car, one knee between the assailant's legs, before he wrenched the knife from the man's hand.

"Move even an inch and I'll crush your balls before I slit your goddamned throat," Reaper growled, holding his own knife against the man's jugular while tossing the other one toward China.

"I just wanted the cunt to give me a blow job," the guy whimpered in terror.

"That would be *lady*," China said from a few feet away, having regained her feet. She held his knife as if she was going to gut him if she got the chance.

"And dragging her into your car is not the way to get one," Reaper pointed out, moving the blade just enough to leave a thin line of blood on the man's throat. "Now, who are you working for?"

"No one," he whined. "I don't work for no one." As he spoke, he tried to grab Reaper's arm. Reaper brought his knee up hard into the man's groin.

"Do that again and you're dead," Reaper told him tightly. "Who do you work for?"

The man choked out, "No one. I swear. I just—"

"Like kidnapping girls and taking them somewhere to play with?"

The guy stayed mute but the look on his face said Reaper had hit the nail on the head.

"So what do I do with you?" Reaper said, as if talking to himself.

"Cut off his balls," China spat.

"One option," Reaper agreed. "Or..." He whipped the attacker around, pushing him face forward against the car. "China, doll, take his belt off of him, please."

"You want me to touch the bastard," she asked, wrinkling her nose in disgust. "Besides, I can't get to the buckle the way you got him."

Wrapping his arm around the man's neck in a chokehold, Reaper pulled him away from the car just enough for China to unbuckle the belt and pull it free. Reaper forced him down on his knees, put one foot on his back and shoved him to the ground. Grabbing the man's arms, Reaper pulled them behind him. He didn't have to tell China what to do. She put the belt around her assailant's wrists and pulled it so tightly he let out a yelp of pain.

"Now can I cut off his balls?" she asked almost gleefully.

"I'll help," the girl she'd been with said, finally joining them.

"No. I have a better idea," Reaper replied. Flipping the man over, he undid the closure on his pants and pulled them off, along with his shoes, leaving him in just his briefs and socks below the waist. Then, using his knife, he cut off his shirt. "Find his wallet and tell me who he is," Reaper told China. When she did, Reaper knelt down, saying, "Nice to meet you, Mr. Langley. I have one thing to say to you before I dispose of you."

"You can't kill me," Langley whimpered. "That's murder."

"You were going to rape her. In my book, that's a hell of a lot worse than murder."

"You can't rape a whore," Langley protested.

Reaper backhanded him. "You heard her. She's a lady. Now apologize." When it looked as if Langley wouldn't, Reaper backhanded him again, saying, "I can keep this up all night — or what's left of it." He paused when the lights of a car lit the end of the street. "Ladies, get into the alley."

The girls did as he'd said while he dragged Langley into the shadow of his vehicle. The car drove past them, the driver apparently unaware there was anyone around. When it was gone, Reaper pulled Langley to his feet and marched him into the alley. After pushing him against the wall, Reaper got right in his face, saying, "I'm not going to kill you — tonight. But if I ever see you in this neighborhood, or hear that you've been trying to pick up any of my friends, I will find you. And" — he smiled evilly — "I know where you live."

With that said, Reaper hauled Langley over to the nearest dumpster, cold-cocked him and tossed him into it.

"Okay, ladies," he said, wiping his hands together. "I suggest you get back to wherever you're staying." He walked over to China and gave her a hug. "You done good."

"I was scared shitless," she admitted, hugging him back. "I was afraid you wouldn't get here in time when I called."

"Someone was watching over us — all of us," he added, smiling at the other girl. "Now off with you while I call the cops and let them know they need to pick up some trash."

* * * *

"Again?" Mike grumbled when he heard the dispatcher say there was a report of a naked man in a dumpster.

Dallas hid a smile. "Sounds like Reaper struck again. Let's take the call."

"I wish he'd just drop them off at the station house," Mike said, as he turned the corner, heading to the dumpsite.

Dallas acknowledged the call and said they'd handle it. He chuckled, saying to Mike, "If we ever see him, suggest it."

"Trust me. I will."

* * * *

"Mike had a suggestion," Dallas said several hours later when he walked into the bedroom.

"About? And you need a shower. You smell," Zack replied, buttoning his shirt.

"I washed up as best as I could. And I wouldn't have had to if someone I know" — he looked sourly at Zack — "would quit dropping people into dumpsters. You need a new place to dispose of them."

"Such as?" Zack asked.

Dallas quickly stripped off his uniform, putting it into the plastic bag that had held it when it came back from the cleaners. "Mike's recommendation is the station house, but somehow I don't think you'll go for that."

Zack nodded. "A bit too risky. I could take them to the landfill."

"Um, no? That would be almost as bad."

"I'll figure out something. Though I do like the symbolism of the dumpsters."

"Yeah, me too," Dallas agreed. "Maybe we can all start carrying hazmat suits with us."

"I doubt the department would go for that," Zack said, knotting his tie.

"It's crooked," Dallas told him.

Zack checked and fixed it.

"Try bowties?" Dallas suggested.

"I am not a bowtie type of guy."

"Nope. You're more the no-tie, turtleneck sort."

Zack laughed. "I don't think that goes with my image as a serious investment counselor. Which, at the moment, I wish I wasn't," he added when Dallas finished undressing.

"Me too. Right now." Dallas stopped on his way to shower long enough to kiss him quite soundly. "But that's life until my schedule changes. Then we'll have all night together."

"When does that happen?"

"With luck, next Monday, if the captain accepts our request. With Mike's wife, Carol, expecting, he wants to be home with her at night."

"Fingers crossed," Zack said. "Okay, I'll see you this evening before you leave for work." They kissed again, then he took off, calling back, "Remember to eat breakfast before you hit the sack or Mrs. Cook will geld you."

* * * *

"The Crystal Room is available on these dates," Mr. Mackie, Zack's client on the board of directors for the Gold Hotel, told him. He handed Zack a typed sheet of paper with the hotel's logo at the top.

Zack took his time, checking the dates against the calendar on his desk. "I'd say the fifteenth or sixteenth. That will give us a good month to pull this together and get the invitations out."

"Speaking from experience, go for the sixteenth. It's a Saturday night, so people will have all day to prepare."

"Makes sense."

"Have you thought of a theme?"

"Making as much money as we can?" Zack replied with a chuckle.

"That's the objective, not a theme."

"I know. I was kidding. Brian started the shelter in 1985 so we were thinking an eighties theme?"

Mackie tapped a finger to his lips. "That would work. Karaoke was just getting a foothold in the States then, so we can do that. We also have a DJ we hire sometimes. I'll see if he might be interested in helping with music. That is, if you're planning on dancing as well as food and drinks."

"Definitely."

"I'd suggest keeping it formal, but in the style of the eighties."

"They had an evening style back then?" Zack asked.

"You don't... Never mind. You weren't even born back then."

"I beg to differ. I was twelve in eighty-five. Of course, at that point, partying was the last thing on my mind." For a moment, Zack was back to the time in his life when he had endured the beatings from his father, which his mother did her best to ignore. It was then that he'd run away, spending the next eight years surviving on the streets until he'd met Brian. He pulled himself back to the present. "I'll need a party planner, I think, and a printer for invitations. Someone to do publicity."

With a smile, Mackie handed him another sheet of paper. "Figured you'd be a bit out of your element, despite the planning you've done so far. These are people the hotel uses. Some work for us. Others have their own businesses. I'm sure I can convince them to give you a break on the costs."

"Thank you," Zack said fervently.

They continued their discussion for a few more minutes then moved on to Mackie's investment portfolio and what needed to be bought and sold to make him more income.

Chapter Eight

Dallas got the news on Friday evening, when he and Mike started their shift, that they were being moved to days starting Monday. To make things even better, they were going on eight hour rather than twelve-hour shifts. He was more than happy about that. It meant he and Zack could actually have some real time to spend together during the week.

Since they'd met four years ago, it often seemed as if they only saw each other in passing—maybe an hour in the morning then about the same in the evening before Dallas headed to work.

Well, other than Sundays and Mondays when I'm off.

On occasion, when he was feeling lonely without Zack around, Dallas wasn't certain Mondays really counted. Sure they did have a couple of hours of quality time between when Zack got home from the office and when he went to bed so he could hit the streets by two as Reaper. But still…

On the other hand, we do have some damned good sex those two days to make up for the rest of the week. I can't really blame him for doing what he does, not after knowing what

his life was like when he was a teen. And I came into our
relationship with my eyes wide open. He let me know almost
from the beginning how he spent his nights, and why.

They had met at a club. One of the few times Zack had actually gone to one, he admitted later. Zack had been sitting at the bar, watching the dance floor while drinking a beer. The only empty seat was next to him and Dallas had grabbed it before anyone else could. They'd begun talking as men do in that situation. Casual conversation about the customers, comparing notes on them. From there, they'd moved on to what they did for a living. Dallas had sort of figured from the way Zack had been dressed, in leathers and a dark turtleneck, that he was maybe a mechanic or a biker. He'd been more than surprised to find out he was actually a businessman. Zack had been equally surprised when Dallas had told him he was a cop. By then, they had finished their beers and Dallas had offered to buy the next round.

"Sorry," Zack had replied, "but I have to leave. I have something I need to do."

Tentatively, Dallas had asked, "Can we maybe get together again sometime? Here or...wherever?"

Zack had seemed to think about it then nodded. "When are you free?"

"Next Sunday." Dallas had smiled ruefully. "I work nights, six to six, if I'm lucky. Later, if I'm not. But I'm off Sundays and Mondays."

"How about lunch, then?"

They'd set a time and place. That had been the start of what at first had been just a friendship with good sex thrown into the mix. In time, they had realized they were falling in love. That was when Zack had finally and fully opened up to Dallas.

They'd been at Zack's house, eating supper on a Sunday evening after having spent the day together.

"I know," Zack said, seemingly out of the blue, "that we have strong feelings for each other." He smiled. "I don't think that's a big secret anymore. But…"

He's going to break it off. Despite what he just said, he's going to end it.

As if he read Dallas' mind, or more probably his expression, Zack shook his head. "I'm not calling it quits – no way, no how. But there are things I haven't told you about myself that I need to if this is going to continue."

"Like…" Dallas tried for a joke. "You secretly spend your nights, while I'm working, roaming the streets looking for victims, because you're really a serial killer?"

Rather than laughing, Zack replied as he stood, "Not quite that bad. Let's go into the living room where we can be more comfortable."

When they were settled on the sofa, Zack remained quiet for so long that Dallas began to wonder how horrible whatever he was going to tell him was.

"I'll start at the beginning. When I was twelve, I left home. Typical story I guess. My father was an angry man and an alcoholic. He took his anger out on me. My mother…" He shrugged. "I guess she thought better me than her, so she kept out of it."

"Damn," Dallas said quietly.

"With nowhere to go, I ended up on the streets. It didn't take me long to realize two things. One, I'd need money to survive. Two, I was still a kid and small enough that I couldn't defend myself." Zack fisted his hands.

Dallas reached to take them, only to have Zack pull them away.

"Let me get through this. Long story short, I learned the ins and outs of survival. The only thing I didn't get involved in was drugs – selling or using. I grew older and bigger. Life became a little easier. I learned how to protect myself and put

that to use helping other kids who needed my...skills with my fists."

"In other words, you kept them safe?" Dallas liked that idea. He was less happy with the thought that Zack had undoubtedly sold himself the way some of the kids did who he saw when he was on patrol. Kids so young they shouldn't even have known what sex was. Kids who grew up knowing the dangers of getting into a stranger's car, or going into an alley with them, to give blow jobs — but did it anyway to stay alive.

"As much as I could," Zack replied. "Then, when I was twenty, I met a man who helped me get off the streets."

"A sugar-daddy?" Dallas asked in dismay.

"Good Lord, no. His name is Brian and he runs a shelter. He took me aside one night when I was crashing there. Told me it was time I decided to do something about my life. It took a while and a lot more talks, but in the end... Well, here I am. A successful businessman."

Dallas slid over to hug him tightly. "Thank you for feeling you could trust me with your story."

"I should have told you a long time ago," Zack said, kissing Dallas' temple. "The thing is..." He pulled away, gazing at Dallas. "There's... Well, I guess you could call it a follow-up to the story."

Something in Zack's expression put Dallas on alert. Warily he asked, "What?"

"Do you know how many homeless kids and adults there are out there who become victims of predators? Not just men who want sex and use them to get it, but the punks who get their jollies from beating up on those who are weak and alone?"

"Given that I'm a cop, I'm well aware of that. I've intervened more than a few times to stop an assault."

"And what happens to the assailant?"

Dallas' mouth tightened. "They walk because their victim is afraid to press charges. I'm sure you know that. The vics are kids who don't want their family to find them. That's why they're out there in the first place."

"Exactly." Zack blew out a long breath. "I'd ask if you can keep a secret, but that sounds so juvenile. Still, it's the best way to put it, especially since you are a cop."

"This doesn't bode well," Dallas replied with a small smile. "Still…unless you're going to confess to breaking the law, I can."

Zack gave him a wry grin. "Define 'the law'… Okay, here goes. About a year ago I decided I had to do something to stop the predators." He took Dallas' hands, holding them tightly. "I spend the early morning hours out looking for them. I step in when I see some bastard attacking a victim and teach them what it's like to have the shit beaten out of you."

Dallas looked at him in shock. "That's vigilantism."

"I know," Zack replied shortly, locking his gaze on Dallas' face. "But it does the job."

Dallas pulled his hands free and got up. He began pacing, occasionally looking at Zack.

Now what do I do? By rights, I should arrest him. He's just confessed to a crime. Multiple crimes, in fact.

"Why don't you call nine-one-one when you see that happening?" Dallas asked.

"To what end? By the time the police get there, if they even do, the assailant is long gone. I suspect you know as well as I do that the homeless are on the bottom of the list when it comes to what cops have to handle."

"Not true," Dallas protested. But he knew Zack was correct. Given the choice of stopping a break-in or a convenience store hold-up, or making a run to some alley to try to catch a thug attacking some homeless person… "All right, I see your point," he admitted. "But damn it, Zack."

"Do you think what I'm doing is wrong? Because I don't."

Dallas dropped down beside him on the sofa, slowly shaking his head. "Legally, yeah, it's very wrong. Morally though…

No, it's not. You're protecting people who can't protect themselves."

Zack put his arm around Dallas, drawing him against his chest. "I hoped... Hell, I prayed that you'd see it that way. Of course, now I've put you in a tight spot. As a cop, can you deal with all this or will you feel the need to walk away, even if you don't turn me in?"

Turning his head to look at Zack, Dallas replied, "I'm not walking away."

"Thank God!" Zack said. "I was so afraid you would, but I had to be honest with you. It's the only way to make what we have work." He smiled ruefully. "Besides which, I'm sure in time you'd start questioning why I slept such weird hours, or had bruises that I couldn't – or wouldn't, I guess – explain."

"How often does that happen?" Dallas asked.

"Coming home looking like I've been through the wars? Not too often. I learned a lot, living on the streets, and I've kept in practice since then. But shit happens – especially when I have to take on more than one punk."

"Do you carry a weapon?"

"A knife, but I try not to use it as more than a threat. I'd rather use my hands and feet. Although if they have something, a lead pipe or a baseball bat, I have no problem taking it away from them then using it to give them a taste of their own medicine."

They talked some more, before going to bed. Their lovemaking that night had held special meaning for both of them, Dallas realized. A bond of trust had been made between them. Trust that neither of them had ever broken.

Now, with his new hours, Dallas wanted to be a part of what Zack – well, Reaper – did. All he had to do was convince Zack to let him.

Chapter Nine

Sunday morning, Zack and Dallas slept in as usual. When the bright sunlight hitting the bed finally woke them, they made slow love, Zack savoring the fact that they could. Then they dressed and went downstairs to eat lunch.

Zack studied Dallas as they ate. He knew something was on his lover's mind. Something that, he thought, had to do with the fact that Dallas would be working days starting tomorrow.

It wasn't until they were rinsing dishes and putting them in the dishwasher that Zack finally asked, "Do you want to talk?"

"Yes," Dallas replied. "But not here. Let's take a walk along the trail."

Zack smiled a bit. "That bad?"

"Not bad. At least, I don't think so." Dallas dried his hands then went to get their jackets, handing Zack his when he got back.

They left the yard through the back gate, locking and arming the security box on it. The day was warm but there was a cool breeze, presaging the arrival of fall in a few weeks. After walking for a quarter of a mile, greeting a few of their neighbors who were also taking advantage of the trail for a Sunday walk or jog, Dallas veered off onto a side path that led to a small pond.

When they got there, he picked up a stone, skipping it across the water. "Still got it," he crowed softly.

"Dallas..." Zack said, coming up beside him. "You're avoiding whatever the subject is."

"Not really. I'm just trying to find the best way to approach it."

"Try directly?"

Dallas nodded, turning to look at him. "I want to help, when you're out as Reaper."

"No way. First off—"

"If you say it's not safe, remember I'm a cop. I'm probably better able to protect myself than you are, which is saying something."

"That wasn't what I was going to say. I know you can. It's the fact that you *are* a cop that presents a problem. People in the Uptown district know you, including some of the SOBs I hunt down. It's the same reason I didn't want you involved looking for the johns who are trying to abduct the kids out there selling themselves. What if someone we go after recognizes you? Your career will go down the tubes."

"People are used to seeing me in uniform." Dallas smiled wryly. "Hell, I walk into a store in street clothes and all I get is this 'I think I know him from somewhere but...' look most of the time."

"That doesn't negate my argument," Zack told him.

"They don't recognize you."

"I don't work in the Uptown. Besides which, even if I did, they'd see me in a suit and tie and... Okay, I'm sort of defeating my argument, saying that."

Dallas grinned. "Yeah, you are." He rested his hands on Zack's hips. "So what do you think?"

"I think it's a stupid idea. But, I guess there's some merit to it."

"It can't be both," Dallas said.

"Oh? It's stupid because you'd be endangering yourself. It has merit since with two of us out there we could scare the shit out of an attacker when we find one and hopefully he'd run rather than facing both of us. And if there's more than one…"

"We're one-on-one with them instead of the way you do it, trying to take one out before the other one can get to you. That way" — he tapped Zack's shoulder — "there's less of a chance of you getting hurt again. Next time a punk's knife might do a lot more damage, or they could have a gun."

"*That* I've never run into."

"Doesn't mean it won't happen."

"You're not to carry," Zack said firmly.

"I'll have a knife, the way you do."

"All right." Zack suddenly smiled, realizing Dallas had talked him into letting him come along. "You're good."

Dallas gave him an innocent look. "It's my Irish charm."

Zack snorted. "You're about as Irish as I am."

"I'll have you know me great-grandfather came over from the auld country," he replied with a very fake Irish lilt.

"And mine came from… Hell, I don't even know where my father came from, other than Hell."

Dallas stroked Zack's cheek. "You're well rid of him. If you'd stayed, I'd never have met you."

"I hope you don't regret it once we're teamed up out there." He kissed Dallas quickly before saying, "Now what will you call yourself?"

After a long moment of thought, Dallas said, "Wrath."

"Hmm...that could work. Sort of alliterative too—Reaper and Wrath."

"We'll strike fear in the hearts of the evil doers."

"I think you do that every day when you're out on patrol."

"I wish," Dallas said almost wistfully. "If I did, there'd be no need for you and me to be out there doing...well, what you've been doing so far."

"True enough, I'm afraid. All right"—Zack put his arm around Dallas' waist—"let's finish our walk then go home, have an early supper and sleep. What time do you have to start in the morning?"

"I'm on seven to four, with Sundays and Thursdays off."

"Not bad. We can be out from one until dawn then come home in time for you to shower and go to work."

"Mess around then shower."

Zack grinned. "Mess around *in* the shower."

"That works."

* * * *

"Ready?" Zack asked, surveying Dallas. His lover was dressed in black, although not in leathers. "You know, what you're wearing makes your blond hair seem to glow."

"My uniform doesn't do that and it's almost as dark. I think you're imagining it."

Zack put his hands on Dallas' shoulders, turning him to face the mirror. "See?"

Dallas just shook his head, muttering, "Imagination." But he took the watch cap Zack handed him and put it on before saying, "Now I'm ready."

They arrived at their destination half an hour later, parking in a lot two doors down from one of the less reputable bars. It, like most of them in the area, catered to working-class men and those who had nothing better to do than spend their days slumped over a beer or whiskey, commiserating with each other about their bad luck and whatever else had pissed them off.

Zack and Dallas had come up with a system for how to proceed. They would each take one side of the street, staying well in the shadows. If one of them spotted trouble, he would let the other know by autodialing — both of them keeping their phones on vibrate. Since they were throwaways, no one else had the numbers.

Dallas felt a bit out of step at first, since his cop's instinct was to look for problems involving someone trying to break into a building or planning a smash-and-grab.

Not that there's much worth grabbing around here except at the liquor stores, and they all have bars on the doors and windows.

He did spot two men at the entrance to an alley, obviously involved in a drug deal. He made note of their faces for future reference, as he'd never seen them before.

Just what I need, a new dealer in the neighborhood.

He moved on, falling into his new persona as he did.

* * * *

Wrath and Reaper had gone three blocks and had just turned a corner onto a side street when Wrath's cell vibrated. He quickly glanced across the street. Reaper, barely discernable in the doorway of a building, was pointing toward two kids. They were young, not more than fifteen, Wrath estimated, and obviously lived on the streets from their dress and demeanor. It took him a moment to get why Reaper was interested in them. Then he realized it was the pair of men — one in a plaid flannel shirt, the other wearing a denim jacket — who appeared to be following the kids that had Reaper on the alert.

When the kids walked into the alley, they took off their battered backpacks. One of them dug into his and handed his companion something. A moment later, there was a flash of a lighter, then Dallas saw the glowing ends of cigarettes before the kids moved deeper into the darkness. The two men stalking them paused at the entrance. Wrath saw one man point, and the other nodded. The sound of low, expectant laughter reached his ears. He suspected the kids didn't hear it since from what he could see of them — primarily the glow of the cigarettes when they turned to talk — they were still walking at a normal pace. Then they disappeared.

They're probably next to a Dumpster.

The two men entered the alley, moving quickly down it. Reaper was a few feet behind them and a minute later, so was Wrath. Like the kids, the men vanished from sight.

Then there was a sharp cry of pain and a shouted, "Don't hurt us!"

Wrath didn't need Reaper to tell him what to do next. They raced the few remaining yards to where the two men were terrorizing the kids. One had the smaller kid shoved against the brick wall. It was obvious he'd already hit the kid once from the blood flowing from the boy's nose. The second one held a length of pipe, about to use it on the taller kid.

"Trying picking on someone your own size," Reaper said. He pulled the flannel-shirted guy off the kid by grabbing the man's arm and swinging him against the Dumpster with a loud crash.

Wrath was already dealing with the other one. He gripped the pipe before the man could finish his swing, twisting the pipe out of his hand. Then, without any remorse, he smashed it across the bastard's elbow. There was a cracking sound, followed by a roar of pain as the man dropped to his knees, cradling his arm.

"Like Reaper said," Wrath growled, "pick on someone your own size."

Reaper had the flannel shirted man's arms twisted behind his back by the time Wrath checked. He forced the guy to his knees in front of the smaller kid he'd been attacking. "Tell him you're sorry for hurting him," Reaper ordered.

"Fuck you," he said defiantly. "Punks like these deserve whatever we do to them. They're like vermin, crawling out of the woodwork."

"And you don't like vermin," Reaper said icily. "Let's see just *how* badly you hate them. I hear this alley is home to a lot of rats. Wrath, did you happen to bring any restraints with you?"

"Nope, plumb forgot to do that. But I bet their belts will work." He quickly unbuckled both belts then yanked them free of the men's pants. "Where are we going to leave him?"

Reaper pulled the Dumpster away from the wall. "We tie his hands to one wheel, his feet to the other…"

"No! God, don't do that," the man blubbered.

"What do you think, guys?" Reaper asked, addressing the two kids.

The one with the bloody nose shivered, shaking his head. "He's a bastard, but…" Then he managed a small smile. "I heard what you did to that one guy. Do it to them."

"But strip them first," the other kid said with a brief grin as he went to join his friend. "You okay," he asked him, digging a less than clean rag from his backpack to wipe away the half-dried blood.

"I'll live," the smaller kid said.

"Dumpster?" Reaper asked Wrath.

Wrath sighed. "Might as well." He hauled the one in the jean jacket to his feet, getting a scream of agony for his efforts. "Kid," he said to the uninjured boy, "how about you take their shoes off for us? I'm sure you can use them, or know someone else who'd appreciate them."

"What about their wallets?" the kid asked.

"Nope, that would be theft."

"And taking their shoes isn't?"

Wrath shrugged. "Technically, maybe, but we'll consider it a donation to a worthy cause. Right?" He glared at the man he was holding.

"Right," he moaned.

"Clothes too?" the other kid asked.

"Not this time," Reaper replied. "We don't want them catching their death of cold." While he spoke, he used one of the belts to bind his captive's hands behind his back.

Wrath shook his head when Reaper tossed him the other belt. "I don't think he'll be climbing out any time soon with his elbow busted."

Reaper nodded. Dragging his prisoner to the edge of the dumpster, he then hoisted him up and toppled him into it. Then, between them, they put the other one in as well.

"Okay, that should do it," Reaper said, closing the cover on the dumpster. "You two"—he looked at the kids—"get your asses over to Off-the-Street."

"Do we have to?"

"Yeah, you do. Clean up, sleep, eat, then you can go on your way." Reaper looked down at the cigarette butts on the pavement. "And quit smoking. It'll kill you."

Not more than fifteen minutes after they'd left the alley, Reaper and Wrath ran into an older homeless boy angrily confronting a girl who looked all of fourteen.

"That's Dalek," Reaper said as they approached the pair. "I'm not sure who the girl is, but knowing Dalek, she's probably one of the ones he protects. And I use the term loosely."

"In other words, he's around when she's turning tricks and keeps her from getting hurt by a john."

"Yep. Let me find out what the problem is."

Wrath hung back while Reaper walked over to join the pair.

"What's the problem, Dal?" Reaper asked, placing his hand on the teen's shoulder.

"This stupid bitch," Dalek replied, shaking his head in obvious disgust.

"I did just like you told me to," the girl replied defiantly.

"No, you didn't, Kalie!"

"I made sure he paid me and that he turned the car off before I got in," she protested.

Dalek rolled his eyes, looking at Reaper. "I bet you know what she didn't do."

"I can guess." Reaper focused his attention on Kalie. "Protection?"

She looked down, scuffing the toe of her worn sneakers on the pavement. "He didn't have any and…and I ran out." She glanced at Dalek. "He said he was clean. Honest. I asked him."

"Girl…" Dalek growled.

"Kalie, look at me," Reaper told her. When she did, he said, "You never, *ever* give a man a blow job without a condom. End of story. It doesn't matter if he offers you twice the going rate. You don't do it."

"That's what I told her," Dalek grumbled. Then he put his arm around Kalie's shoulders. "If you won't listen to me, listen to him. He knows everything."

Reaper chuckled. "Not sure about that, Dal."

"Sure you do. You're Reaper."

Kalie stared up at Reaper, seemingly awestruck. "For reals? You're him?"

"I am," Reaper acknowledged. "Be that as it may, you have to listen when Dal tells you what to do. He's been around long enough to get it." Returning his attention to Dalek, Reaper said, "Take her to the free clinic to get tested. She's probably fine, but it's not worth taking a chance."

"Yeah, I know. I will."

"Do you have a safe place to crash?"

Dalek snorted. "This is me. Of course I do. We got a squat that's where no one can find us."

"All right. I'd suggest you head there now before you get busted." As he said that, Reaper pointed to a squad car two blocks away, coming toward them.

"Got ya," Dalek said as he began steering Kalie into the alley behind them. "And thanks, man."

* * * *

"Are you all right with what we did tonight?" Zack asked, when he and Dallas got home. He had refrained from asking before then, wanting to give Dallas a chance to process everything. Knowing what to expect and actually being involved in it could, he knew, be two very different things, especially since Dallas was a cop.

"I shouldn't be," Dallas replied. "If I'd been on my own, I'd have arrested those two punks who were terrorizing the kids in the alley. Not that spending a night in a holding cell would have taught them anything."

"And they'd have lawyered up and been out by morning."

"Yeah, I know. They'd have gotten a slap on the wrist when they got in front of a judge, despite my testimony, because the kids wouldn't have been willing to come to court to testify against them, even if we could have found them again." Dallas blew out a long breath. "So, yeah, I was okay with what we did to them." He smiled dryly. "Just like I always was when you did it on your own. Well, other than having to dig a perp out of a dumpster. At least this time it'll be one of the other guys who gets that lovely job."

"What about the rest of it?"

Dallas grinned. "I think that man just about shit his pants when you offered to take him into that diner and buy him a good meal. He was dead sure you were going to roust him for whatever change he'd managed to get, begging outside of it." Turning serious again, he said, "I guess I didn't realize that you did more than just take care of the predators who prey on the street kids. How come you never told me that?"

Zack shrugged. "It never came up."

"Zack…" Dallas shook his head. "What you did for…umm, Dalek and Kalie? That was a good thing. Now if you could only convince them there are better ways to earn money."

"I wish. I'd love to do that for all the kids out there selling themselves, but that won't happen. When you're in that position, you do what you must to survive."

"Someone needs to go around handing out condoms to them."

"Someone does. Most of the shelters have outreach people who distribute food, water and condoms to the kids. The problem is, getting them understand how important it is to make the johns use them. Like Kalie tonight. The john told her he was clean and, foolishly, she believed him. Or, I guess, she wanted to because she needed the money."

"So from now on, we carry condoms with us when we're out there."

Zack smiled, hugging him tightly. "We will."

"For now, however," Dallas said with a sigh, "I need to shower and get ready for work."

Zack glanced at the time before saying, "We'll shower together and…" He gave Dallas a fiery kiss. "Work off the stress from tonight."

"I think I can handle that."

Chapter Ten

Dallas spent the next few days trying to get used to his new hours for work since his body clock was adjusting to getting up in the morning, rather than going to bed. That, coupled with spending the early morning hours on the streets with Zack, left him tired and a bit grumpy. Even having just had Thursday off didn't do much to alleviate it since Zack still had to go into the office.

Mike, on the other hand, was a happy camper. "I'm actually getting to spend quality time with Carol, and pretty soon with my son too."

"If we don't get switched back to nights when the next shift assignments come up," Dallas grumbled.

"Bite your tongue." Mike, who was driving as usual, made the turn onto a side street. "You know that vigilante guy, Reaper?"

"Presumed vigilante," Dallas pointed out.

"Okay. Presumed. Anyway, rumor has it he has a partner now."

"Seriously," Dallas replied, feigning surprise. "So pretty soon they'll be making us obsolete."

Mike snorted. "Not from what the captain said at roll call."

"Which was?"

"Don't tell me you fell asleep while he was talking. Damn, Dallas."

Dallas grinned. "Nope. Was just resting my eyes — and my ears."

"Man, you have to stop staying up so late watching bad cop movies — or is it action shows?"

A bit of both, but not the way he thinks. "Actually, it's horror movies. I'm still having trouble getting a full night's sleep."

"You need some hot sex. That'll knock you out like that." Mike snapped his fingers.

"First I'd need to find someone to have it with."

"Hit up a couple of clubs. There's got to be men out there who are turned on by the idea of screwing a cop."

"Maybe I'm the screwer, not the screwee," Dallas replied, winking.

"TMI," Mike grumbled before getting back to what he'd been saying originally. "Anyway, there's a BOLO out on this Reaper guy, and the captain wants everyone gathering any information they can on him and whoever's helping him."

Just what we need. "Yeah, I saw the BOLO. Not that the day shift will have much luck with that, since he apparently only works nights, or more specifically, very early in the morning."

"Which we know from dealing with the aftermath." Mike chuckled. "Another nice perk of working days. We don't have to dumpster dive for his… Well, not sure they're victims, considering why he chooses them."

"Definitely not victims. Perps would be my description. And they deserve what he does to them."

"Don't tell me you agree with what he's doing."

Dallas shrugged. "He's helping clean up the streets. Leaving us time to worry about the important things, like B&Es, holdups and what have you."

"Traffic stops," Mike added as he turned on the lights and flashers to let the driver of a car that had just run a red light know to pull over.

"That too." *I have to let Zack know about the BOLO.*

Mike pulled up behind the car when it came to a stop at the curb.

* * * *

"Just what we don't need," Zack said upon hearing Dallas' news about the BOLO. He finished hanging up his suit and shirt as he thought about it. "Exactly what are they looking for?"

"A man dressed in black and leathers, with dark, possible black, medium-length hair, probably accompanied by a second man. No description on him so far."

"Good. Let's keep it that way."

"You know," Dallas said, as he took off his uniform shirt, "you could start wearing something else."

"Silver armor?" Zack asked, smirking.

"No, you nut. Though it would suit you." He folded the shirt, adding it to the pile for the cleaners. "There is another option. We do a one-eighty and dress as if we're homeless. It wouldn't be as threatening, but there would still be the element of surprise and we'd be a hell of a lot harder to spot."

Zack nodded slowly. "I thought about that at the beginning, but" — he chuckled — "my need for theatrics won out."

Dallas snorted. "Of course it did, but I think it's time to shelve that and go for the practical." By then, he had his pants off and went to set them on the pile as well. He turned back to find Zack right in front of him, a lascivious look on his face. "We should eat and get to bed," Dallas muttered.

"I'm aiming for getting to bed then eating afterward," Zack replied. "Think we should do that?" He cupped Dallas' face, giving him a swift kiss, followed by a slower, deeper one, thus muffling whatever Dallas' answer might have been.

"Bed…good…" Dallas managed to get out when the kiss ended.

Since it had been his suggestion, Zack made quick work of tumbling Dallas onto the bed and stripping him of his briefs.

"Now what to do with you." Zack sat back on his heels, eyeing his lover. "Looks like this" — he stroked his fingers lightly up and down Dallas' already semi-erect cock — "needs some attention of the oral kind."

"No…kidding… So…?"

Zack winked. "In a moment, love. First…" He tweaked each of Dallas' nipples, well aware of the effect it would have. He smiled when Dallas' cock hardened perceptively. "Better. But…"

"Damn it, Zack!"

"Aw, getting impatient?" Zack grinned before getting down to business. He took Dallas' cock into his mouth, laving it with his tongue to bring Dallas right to the edge then releasing him. Despite Dallas' groan of dismay, Zack waited until his lover had calmed somewhat then began his exquisite torture again. This time, he partially swallowed Dallas' member, after circling the base with two fingers to keep him from coming.

Reaper

"You are being…" Dallas growled even as he arched, thrusting his cock deeply into Zack's throat. "A…damned…brat."

After chuckling to torment his lover even more, Zack finally moved away, still keeping his fingers where they were. Kneeling, he said, "I'm too old to be a brat."

"Bet me." Putting his hands on Zack's shoulders, Dallas pulled himself up, meshing his lips to Zack's in a passionate, heated kiss, fucking his lover's mouth with his tongue. Then he eased Zack back onto the bed. "Legs up."

"Is that an order, Officer?"

Dallas smirked. "You bet it is."

While Zack complied, Dallas got the lube, generously greasing two fingers. Settling between his thighs, Dallas pushed one finger into Zack's waiting hole. He found the sweet spot and began to torment Zack, stroking then pausing.

"You are so dead if you do that one more time."

"Do you know what happens when you threaten a cop?" Dallas asked, pushing the second finger in to stretch Zack's entrance.

"I'm screwed?"

"That would be one result," Dallas agreed. He eased his fingers out and applied a thick dollop of lube to his cock, slathering it from the base to the bulbous head.

Zack watched him in anticipation of what was to come. When instead of entering him, Dallas leaned over to lick the pre-cum from Zack's leaking slit, Zack gasped in surprise. "You are going to drive me insane." He moaned.

"I was considering it," Dallas admitted, chortling. "But I'm not sure I have enough willpower not to come while I do." With that said, he pressed the head of his cock to Zack's hole and thrust inside him.

Zack let out a groan, Dallas paused, and Zack arched up, taking his lover's cock halfway in. "Now, screw me," he panted.

"With pleasure." Dallas thrust all the way in before wrapping his hand around Zack's throbbing cock.

"Yes," Zack barely got out as he rode Dallas' hand while his lover fucked him into oblivion. Pleasure mounted, Zack's balls tightened, and he exploded, his cum splattering both their chests as his orgasm shattered him. Almost at the same moment, Dallas let out a cry of release that echoed through the room.

"I'll never get enough of this—or of you," Zack said as he gathered Dallas into his arms a few moments later. He could feel his lover's tremors—that matched his own as they came down from their sexually induced high—and gently kissed him. "I love you, with all my heart."

"I love you as well," Dallas whispered against his lips. "Always and forever."

Chapter Eleven

Reaper stumbled down the street with Wrath right beside him. He bit back a laugh when Wrath tripped then cursed a non-existent crack in the sidewalk.

"Ain't no crack there, man. Sidewalk's smooth as a baby's bottom."

"Damned lumpy baby then," Wrath retorted, wrapping his arms around himself.

They continued on their way, glancing down alleys when they passed them, as if looking for the right one to crash in. Reaper was dressed in well-worn jeans, with a blue flannel shirt that looked like it had come out of the nearest dumpster. He also wore a dirty gray T-shirt and battered tennis shoes. He had an old baseball cap with a bent brim settled crookedly on his head. Wrath had on multi-patched tan khakis, a green collarless shirt and a holey hoodie with the hood pulled up over a blue watch cap.

In front of them was a small park, lit only by the half-moon above it and one tired lamppost at the back edge. As they began to walk past, they heard taunting voices.

"Problem," Reaper said sotto voce. He inched his way into the shadows along the side of the park with Wrath right behind him. Ahead by the lone bench, they saw three well-dressed, somewhat inebriated teens. Beyond them, barely discernable, was a raggedy homeless man of indeterminable age. His shopping cart lay on its side beside the bench, the contents spread across the ground.

One of the teens picked up something that had fallen from the cart and threw it at the derelict. The second teen did the same and said in disgust, "Who'd wear this?"

The third, and bulkiest, teen watched for a moment then shoved the homeless man off the bench onto the pile of clothing, tattered blankets and other items. The man curled up, covering his head and yelping when one of the teens grabbed something heavy from the pile and hit him with it. He cried out again when one of the teens kicked him.

"Having fun, boys?" Reaper asked from a few feet away.

"Look, guys, this piece of shit has a friend," the biggest teen said, spinning around to face him. "Where's *your* shopping cart? I thought all you people had them."

Getting in the teen's face, Reaper growled, "Like all you punks have no brains?"

"Oh boy, we have a brave one," the teen crowed, making a grab for Reaper's arm. Suddenly, he was on the ground with Reaper towering over him.

"You like kicking people when they're down?" Reaper asked. "Well, turnabout is fair play, wouldn't you say?" He landed a hard kick to the teen's hip.

Wrath came into view. He reached for the smallest teen, who darted out of the way. The third teen picked up a thick stick from the pile beside the cart, holding it threateningly.

"I dare you," Wrath told him, smirking.

The kid lunged at him, swinging the stick. Wrath ducked, kicking out his leg to trip the teen. As the boy started to fall, Wrath grabbed his arm, twisting it behind his back. Wrath let out a whoof of air when the smallest one tackled him. If Wrath hadn't been holding the other teen, he would have fallen. As it was, Wrath spun him around by his arm, using him as a battering ram to knock the small boy down. A popping sound, followed by a scream of pain, let Wrath know he'd dislocated the teen's shoulder in the process.

By then, Reaper had pulled the bulky one to his feet. "If I was you," Reaper told him, "I'd gather up my friends and get the hell out of here before we turn all of you into pulp."

The punk looked for a moment as if he was going to argue the point, so Reaper backhanded him.

"If we ever see the three of you hassling the homeless again," Reaper said angrily, "what we did to you tonight will seem like child's play. Understand?"

The teen muttered, "If we don't take care of you first," but he backed away fearfully. Then he and the other one helped their companion, who was crying with pain, out of the park.

"Thank you, thank you," the homeless man said, staggering to his feet. He rubbed his shoulder, where the can had hit it, wincing.

"Are you going to be okay?" Wrath asked with concern.

"Had worse than this done to me," he replied. He thanked him when Wrath righted the shopping cart, and with Wrath's and Reaper's help, he got everything back into it.

"You take care," Reaper said. "And get something to protect yourself."

"Had that stick, but they surprised me," the man told him.

Reaper nodded. "A piece of rebar works better, but you have to keep it with you when you crash, not in the cart."

The guy smiled wryly. "I'll remember that, for next time."

After saying goodbye, Reaper and Wrath left the park. They walked half a block before Reaper felt his phone — the one he was using for China and her friends to contact him — vibrate. He dug it out.

Zip here. Brown Chevy, missing hubcap, Park & 6th.

Reaper texted back.

Thanks. Coming. Keep an eye on it if you can.

He got one back a moment later.

Gonna try.

"We've got a date with another one of the predators."

"The ones going after the girls?" Wrath asked.

"Yep. Let's move it."

It took them five minutes, going at a dead run, to get to the address Zip had given Reaper. The boy wasn't in sight, but a girl stepped out of the shadows. She looked puzzled for a second then asked tentatively, "You Reaper? You don't look like what they said."

"I am," Reaper told her.

"Okay. Zip and Colly took off that way." She pointed. "Said to tell you the car was heading toward Seventh, where some of the girls hang out, moving slow."

"Thanks."

"Cruising for a victim, I suspect," Wrath said as they walked quickly toward Seventh.

"No shit." Reaper saw Zip at the end of the block and started toward him, saying, "Is he still around?"

"Who the hell are you?" Zip asked.

Reaper chuckled. "The new, improved Reaper."

"Aw shit, man. Why? You ain't nearly as scary like that."

"I'll tell you later. Right now, where's the car?"

"Around the corner. The dude pulled up and parked but he didn't do nothing yet 'cause none of the girls approached him."

"How many girls?" Reaper asked as they started walking.

"Two. Colly's keeping an eye on them."

"Colly being?"

Zip grinned. "My guy."

"Okay. Good that he's there, but let's hope he didn't scare away our perp." Reaper got into character again, shuffling onto the side street. Ahead, about halfway down, he saw the girls and a skinny kid who was maybe seventeen, if that.

Hardly someone who'll terrorize the guy we're looking for.

Unfortunately, those three were the only people in sight. The car was gone. With a sigh of disgust, Reaper led the way to the kids with Zip and Wrath right behind him.

"There wasn't nothing we could do to keep him here," the boy said to Zip while looking askance at Reaper and Wrath. "She" — he pointed to one of the girls — "went over to talk to him but…" He shrugged. Then his expression brightened. "I got the plate number."

"Excellent," Reaper said.

"What's he? Undercover cop?" one of the girls, standing in a shadowed doorway with her companion, asked Zip.

"Nope. He's one of the good guys," Zip replied.

Reaper chuckled, glancing at Wrath. "Nothing wrong with cops," Reaper told them.

The girl just snorted softly.

Returning his attention to Zip's boyfriend, Reaper asked for the plate number. The kid handed him a torn scrap of paper, saying, "You think you can find him? He's really…weird. Kept eyeing Missy like she was primo and he wanted some of her, but was afraid to make the first move. Then, when she went to the car he…" The kid looked at the girl Reaper figured was Missy.

"He said he wanted me to come with him behind the building. I was like, no way," the girl told him, coming over to stand by Colly. "I said he should turn off the car, then I'd get in and blow him. He waved a fifty at me and damn I was tempted, but I heard about other girls going missing and Colly said he could be the guy, so I told him to fuck off and he got real pissed. Tried to grab my arm, but I moved away fast." She grinned weakly. "Then he took off."

"Can you describe him?" Reaper asked.

"Uh-huh. Red hair, mustache, maybe…thirtyish? Had muscles. I mean *big* ones. Here." She put her hand on Reaper's bicep. "Least they looked like they'd be big. He was wearing a sweatshirt. Blue with a logo on it."

"Do you remember what it said?"

She shook her head. "It was too dark and the letters were black."

"All right." Reaper asked the other girl if she had anything to add.

She shook her head.

"You all did a great job," he told them. "Now Wrath and I have more to work with."

Zip looked at Wrath. "That's what you call yourself?" He grinned. "Like the wrath of God my mom always threatened me with?"

Wrath nodded. "Sorta. But I don't have lightning bolts."

"Huh?"

"Saw that in a picture. God with lightning coming from his fingers," Wrath explained.

"Man, that's cool."

"Is, isn't it? But not something I can do."

"Bummer."

Reaper shook his head then suggested the kids head back to wherever they crashed, especially Missy. "And watch your backs. He's probably gone, but there's no sense taking chances. We'll tag along behind you for a few blocks, just to be sure he's not hanging around."

The teens nodded. Zip and Colly walked on either side of the girls, obviously intending to keep them safe if the predator reappeared.

"They're very protective of each other," Wrath commented, as he and Reaper followed, keeping their distance.

"Yeah. Most street kids are—when they can be. And if they're not loners."

"Like you were?" Wrath asked softly.

"Most of the time, I was," Reaper replied. "That was just me."

"Still is," Wrath said. "Most of the time."

* * * *

"I'll pass the license-plate number and the guy's description on to vice," Dallas said once he and Zack were back at the car.

They'd already stashed the majority of their clothing disguises in the trunk.

"On what grounds?" Zack asked.

"That one of my informants told me someone had tried to grab his on again, off again girlfriend and she told him as much as she remembered about the bastard."

"Better yet," Zack said as he started the car, "run a search on the plate to find out who he is."

Dallas nodded, but didn't look happy. "And take care of him ourselves? All we have is the word of those kids that he's the right man. There must be dozens of cars fitting the description of the one he drives."

"With a missing hubcap?"

"Okay, that narrows the odds some, but with no proof..."

"Just find out who he is. We can figure out what to do afterward."

With a sigh, Dallas said, "Yeah, okay, I'll do it."

Chapter Twelve

Since he was off on Thursday, Dallas didn't get a chance to run the license plate until Friday. What he found out unsettled him. The car belonged to one Jeffery Kinsley, M.D. Dallas. He looked him up and found that the man was a plastic surgeon with offices in a very modern and very pricey high-rise building in one of the wealthier areas of the city. Another check told Dallas the car was one of three owned by the doctor. The other two were an MG and a Lexus, both this year's.

So why drive the old one?

He shook his head at the stupidity of his question.

* * * *

"So that no one will think he's anything more than a guy looking for a fast hookup," Zack said several hours later when Dallas had given him the information. "Considering who he is, that's not in the least surprising."

"You know him?" Dallas asked.

"I know *about* him. He's fairly prominent within his circle—family man, a large donor to some of the more prestigious charities, held in high regard by his colleagues. His list of patients includes the wives of some of my clients."

"Then why the hell is he trying to abduct girls off the street?"

"That, my dear man, is the question." Zack took a bite of his pasta, since they were eating dinner while having the discussion. He waved his fork at Dallas after a moment's thought. "Do we have a home address for him? And as far as that goes, a photo or two? We do want to make certain he matches the description that Missy gave us, just so we know someone else in his household isn't borrowing the car."

"I have both. I emailed his driver's license photo to myself." He shook his head when Zack started to get up. "It's not going anywhere. You can see it after dinner."

"Don't go all bossy on me," Zack grumbled.

"Me?" Dallas chuckled when Zack nodded. "Question. If you know who he is, why don't you already know what he looks like?"

"Because I've never actually met him. What I know, I've heard from my clients talking about him and from articles in the social section of the newspaper."

"Okay. I know I've never run into him. But then, I doubt he's the kind of person who makes it a habit to come into the Uptown district, except maybe to go through it to a downtown restaurant or the theater."

"If we're right, he comes there for something else as well. Does the man in the photo have a mustache and red hair?"

"Nope. Brown hair. However, he is in his thirties. Thirty-nine according to the license. He doesn't look that old though. Hard to tell if he's muscular, of course."

"We'll print it off and take it with us to show Missy. She might or might not recognize him from that."

"I'll make a copy first and play around with it. Give the guy red hair and the mustache to match what she told us. Hell, we'll do a search to see if we can find any photos online. If he's that well known, there have to be some somewhere."

An hour later, Dallas had found several pictures of Jeffery Kinsley. In none of them did he have red hair, but one of them showed him with a small mustache. "Not that it'll help much," he said. "If—and I'm beginning to think it's a big if—the man Missy saw is Kinsley, I'd say he's wearing a wig and fake mustache."

"Using the theory that having one feature that stands out draws attention to it, so a witness is less likely to remember the rest of his face," Zack replied with a nod. "Makes sense to me. Print the newest one out, then we'll get some sleep."

"Now who's being bossy?" Dallas asked with a grin. He did as Zack had asked, however, then closed down the computer.

They were in bed by seven, and would be up again at one in the morning to get ready for their almost nightly trip to the rundown area of the city that they patrolled.

* * * *

"Slow night for once," Wrath commented, buttoning the tattered coat he was wearing to block the chill.

Reaper nodded, scanning an alley they were passing. "It would be nice if it stayed that way."

"How are we going to find Missy? Presuming she's out and about tonight."

Reaper thumbed toward three kids leaning against the wall of a derelict building before going over to talk to them. The girl looked at him askance then broke into a wide grin.

"Going native on us, Reaper?" Raven asked.

"Protective coloring," he replied.

"Bet I know why," one of the boys, who Reaper knew went by the name Dabby, said. "Cops looking for you."

"Now why would they be doing that?" Reaper said, one corner of his mouth cocking up with amusement.

"'Cause they don't like... Hell, what's that word the cop used?" Dabby looked at his friends.

"Vigilantes," Raven told him before looking at Reaper with a worried frown. "They *are* looking for you and" — her gaze went to Wrath—"him too, maybe?"

"So I heard," Reaper replied, smiling dryly.

"Sucks," Raven said. "You were sexy in the leathers."

"Yeah, well... Anyway, back to why I'm here right now. Do any of you know a girl who calls herself Missy?"

"Yep," the third kid said. "Saw her earlier tonight. She was hanging with Kip and Colly over by Grant Middle School."

"Thanks. I'll check it out. And if you see her, tell her we need to talk. Okay? I'll be... You know the building on Tyler that used to be a print shop?" When the trio nodded, Reaper said, "Tell her I'll go by there on-and-off tonight and to wait there. It's important."

"Will do," Raven replied.

"Good. Catch you later, I'm sure. And behave." Reaper laughed when the three teens looked at him as if he was crazy, then he and Wrath took off, heading toward the school.

Luck was with them. As the school came in sight, they saw a small group of kids in the playground lit dimly by a streetlight on the corner. The boys seemed to be shooting baskets with, Reaper decided when he got closer, a half-inflated soccer ball. "Don't get much bounce with that, do you?" he called out.

He and Wrath pushed open the gate in the fence surrounding the playground.

"Got a better idea?" an older boy replied defiantly as he turned to see who had asked.

"Yep. Stop by a gas station and use their air machine."

The boy snorted. "Only one around here ain't got one. You gotta be in the 'burbs for that. And who are you to be telling me what to do, old man?"

"Shush, Vince," Zip said, coming up to the boy. "That's Reaper."

"No way! From what I've heard, Reaper's one tough-looking dude. That guy" — Vince pointed at Reaper — "couldn't knock out a fly by the look of him."

"Don't judge by appearances," Reaper said, joining them. He held out his hand. Cautiously, Vince took it and, seconds later, he was face down on the ground with him arm twisted behind his back. Reaper released him immediately, helping him get to his feet again.

"Damn, man, can you show me how to do that?" Vince asked hopefully.

"Later, maybe. Right now I need to talk to Missy."

"About what?" Missy wanted to know, coming over from the edge of the playground where she and two other girls had been watching the guys.

"Let's go where there's more light and I'll show you."

One of the other boys snickered. "Usually a dude wants to go into a dark corner for that."

Reaper rolled his eyes as he led the way to the corner of the yard by the streetlight. After opening his battered backpack, he took out a folder with the pictures of Kinsley that Wrath had printed out. Showing them to

Missy, Reaper asked, "Is this the man you told me about?"

"Could be," she said hesitantly as she looked through them. "This one's pretty close."

Reaper saw it was the one where Wrath had given the man red hair.

"Mustache is wrong, though," Missy told him. "The dude had a bigger one, you know." She ran her fingers over her upper lip to show how big.

"Okay." Reaper put his hand over the lower part of the man's face in the photo. "Now what about the eyes and forehead? As much as you can remember, are they the same?"

"Yeah and no." She closed her eyes then opened them and looked again. "The guy had lines here, like he frowned a lot. And crow's feet."

"You actually remember all that in the brief time you saw him?"

"Uh-huh. Because I thought it didn't fit with his muscles and the sweatshirt. Like he was trying to look younger than he was. And I was trying to remember, in case it was the guy Colly said was grabbing girls like me." She glanced guiltily at Reaper. "I should have told you that the first time, but it wasn't 'til you showed me these that I really remembered, if you know what I mean."

"I do, and it's okay."

"Could the man you saw be this man's older brother?" Wrath asked her.

"Yeah, maybe." She shrugged. "Or these old pictures."

Wrath chuckled. "There is that."

"Anything else you remember, now that you've seen the photos?" Reaper asked her. "Anything at all."

Missy shook her head. "I wish there was, but that's it."

"Well, it's better than we had before."

Zip asked the obvious question, that Missy hadn't. "You know who he is?"

"We think we do, thanks to Colly getting the plate number of the car. And now, with Missy saying the man she saw could be him…" Reaper replied.

"So you're going after him?" Colly asked, sounding excited.

"Possibly. First we need to make certain he *is* the man and that it's not, like Wrath suggested, an older brother or perhaps a relative."

"Just like in the movies."

Reaper chuckled. "Well, sort of, Colly. A bad B-movie."

"Cool."

"Can we get back to our game now?" Vince asked.

"Have at it," Reaper told him. "And by the way, you know the warehouse on Third? Check behind it. I think I saw an air pump that they use for the trucks."

"Thanks, man. I will." Vince tossed the deflated ball up and caught it. "Yeah, this only works for shooting baskets."

The boys went back to their game, with the girls leaning on the fence to watch, as Reaper and Wrath walked out of the playground.

"So," Wrath said, "was it Kinsley or someone else?"

"Right now I'd say it's fifty-fifty. I think I'll see if I can make an appointment to talk to him about getting rid of my frown lines."

Wrath studied him, shaking his head. "I'm not sure he'll buy that. They're barely noticeable."

"I'm egotistical. I want Botox injections. Even if he says I don't need them, it will give me a chance to meet him up close and get a feel for what he's like."

"I guess that would work." Wrath stopped talking, his gaze going to two men walking half a block ahead of them. One man paused at the entrance to an alley, shook his head a moment later, saying something to his companion before they moved on. "Looking for trouble?" Wrath said quietly.

"Perhaps. So we'll keep an eye on them."

Chapter Thirteen

Zack did call Dr. Kinsley's office on Monday and managed to get an appointment for Wednesday, thanks to a cancellation. After arriving at the doctor's office, the receptionist handed him forms to fill out.

"I'm only here to talk to him," Zack pointed out.

"I'm sorry, but it's procedure," she told him.

He did as she'd requested, then he waited, as was the norm when dealing with doctors, using his time to call a client to discuss one of the woman's holdings.

He was so involved that he wasn't aware the doctor was there until he heard him say, "I'll have to remember that for my own stocks."

Looking up, Zack saw the man he thought might be the predator standing in front of him.

"Good morning. I'm Dr. Kinsley," he said, holding out his hand.

Zack shook it, replying, "I'm Zack Ward."

"Let's go into my office to talk," Kinsley suggested, as he took the forms the receptionist handed to him.

Once seated across from each other at the large, modern desk, Kinsley studied Zack. Zack returned the favor for a moment before looking at the pictures at one side of the desk. There were two in silver frames. One was obviously of Kinsley and his family, a lovely blonde woman and two children who Zack estimated were ten and twelve. The other showed an older couple, seated, with three men standing behind them. One was Kinsley. The other two were virtual carbon copies of him except for hair coloring. The oldest one, probably mid-forties Zack guessed, had dark brown hair. The middle brother — or at least Zack presumed that the men were brothers — had hair that was much more auburn, verging on red. Kinsley, the youngest of the three, had light brown hair.

"Nice looking family," Zack said. "Where did the red hair come from?" He tapped the picture of the brothers.

"My grandfather on my father's side." Kinsley chuckled. "My father used to tease Mother that she must have had an affair with the milkman. When Peter was a kid, it was really red. But enough of family. Exactly what are you looking for, Mr. Ward, in terms of plastic surgery?"

"Please, call me Zack." He leaned back then, as if embarrassed to be talking about it. "Botox. Maybe. To take care of these." He brushed one finger over what he knew were barely visible frown lines above his nose.

"Trying to get a jump on aging?" Kinsley asked with a smile. He glanced at the forms Zack had filled out. "As an investment counselor, I would think age would be a recommendation, not a draw back. It shows you have experience."

"Trying to talk yourself out of a patient?" Zack asked with a grin.

"Not really. But I do believe in honesty. Only someone looking closely would be aware of them. There are doctors who advocate getting Botox injections at an early age, to prevent the wrinkles from ever forming." He pressed his fingers together. "I'm not of that school. The shots are expensive and need to be given every three to four months before the muscles reawaken."

Zack whistled softly. "I should have done my research."

Kinsley smiled in agreement. "Most people don't, I'm afraid."

"I guess I'll have to think more about this before coming to a decision. Thank you for being frank with me."

"No, Frank would be my oldest brother. I'm Jeffery," Kinsley replied with a laugh. "Bad joke, I know." He stood, offering his hand. "Please call if you do decide Botox injections are what you want."

After shaking Kinsley's hand, Zack said, "I'll definitely think about what you said, before deciding one way or the other," and left the office. When he stopped at the front desk to ask how much he owed, he was told that the initial consultation was free. He thanked the woman and took off to go back to work.

* * * *

"Dr. Kinsley seems like a nice man," Zack told Dallas that evening. "He does, however, have a brother with auburn hair, and they look alike. In fact, all three brothers do."

"Did you get names?" Dallas asked, lifting the cover of the crockpot to see what Mrs. Cook had fixed them for supper.

"Yep. Peter and Frank. Peter's the redhead."

"Okay. Let's eat then run an online search on him."

"How was your day?" Zack asked him, getting the plates from the table to dish out the chicken and dumpling for each of them.

"We handled a bad crash on the highway. The two cars... If they hadn't been different colors you'd have thought it was one car, they were so damned crushed together." Dallas got beers from the fridge. "Thank God the ambulance arrived at the same time we did. One driver was still alive, although barely. The other one..." He shook his head. "He didn't make it, and they had to cut his passenger out of the car. She's in intensive care, as is the other driver."

"Any idea what caused the accident?"

"Yeah. Stupidity. A witness said the dead driver was on his cell phone. When the hell will people learn?"

"When they ban driving and texting, I suppose."

"We had to tell the widow." Dallas sighed dismally. "That never gets easier. Never."

Zack gave him a tight hug. "I know. I know."

They ate in silence for a few minutes.

Dallas told him with a small smile, "We did get a cat out of a tree."

"I thought that was the fire department's job."

"Usually is, but the poor kid responsible for it being there flagged us down. He was beside himself. He said his dog chased it up the tree and his mother would be pissed. Luckily, it was a small tree and Mike's good with cats. He managed to cajole it within reach then grabbed it. Turns out it belonged to the lady in the house next door and somehow it was able to get out. She gave us all cookies as a reward—even the kid."

"Waistline, Dallas," Zack said with a grin.

"Worked them off chasing down a couple of punks who tried to tag a storefront."

"As the joys of the life of a cop."

"Tell me about it."

With supper finished and the dishes in the washer, they got fresh beers and went to do an online search for Peter Kinsley. Dallas found several men with that name, but only one who fit the age parameters.

"He's a city bus driver. A bit of a comedown from what his brother does." Going onto Facebook, Dallas typed in the name. Again, there were several men using that name. All but two had profile pictures showing either twentysomethings or businessmen. Of the two who didn't, one picture was of a dog. The other Peter Kinsley had a naked shot of a back from the waist up, well muscled and tattooed. The man's hair was red.

Dallas checked the one with the dog and quickly eliminated him. He was eighteen, if his information was to be believed, but looked all of sixteen. Then he went to the page of the tattooed man. He didn't have many friends, and the majority of them were male. The pictures posted on his page were of scantily dressed, well-endowed, females. Below each picture were comments by Kingsley and his friends that were very sexually demeaning.

"This guy has a problem," Zack muttered. "I wish there was a front view of him so we could be certain he's our Peter Kinsley."

"He has several albums. Let's see what we come up with."

"But not right now. We have to get to bed. It's already almost seven."

Dallas held up a finger and signed out. Then he signed in again, which took him a couple of minutes and a few keystrokes. Once he was successful, he went back to Kinsley's page, opening the photos section. He clicked on an album that, from the cover picture of a pipe wrench, should have held photos of plumbing equipment, not barely dressed women. "This it tagged 'Tools I use on the job', and it's available only to his friends," he said. "So maybe there's a picture of him working." He was wrong. Opening it, he found shots of girls, none of them over the age of consent. They were posed provocatively, wearing only thongs, if that.

"They are not doing that willingly, despite the smiles," Zack said angrily. "Look at the despair in their eyes."

"Our missing girls?" Dallas asked.

"You had better believe it," Zack growled in reply. "How the hell does he get away with posting them here?"

"Like I said, it's tagged so that only he and his friends can see it."

"Then how did you get into it?"

"I'm clever," Dallas replied with a grin. He pointed to the name he'd signed in with. It belonged to one of Kinsley's friends. "A trick one of our computer experts in the department taught me. It doesn't always work, but when it does, you can find out a lot of interesting things about suspects."

"Makes me glad I'm not on Facebook," Zack replied dryly. "Now, shall we get some sleep then go looking for Mr. Peter Kinsley?"

"Yep." Dallas got off the Internet and closed down the computer. "The question is," he said as they walked upstairs, "how did he get hold of his brother's car?"

"Borrowed it, or he has the use of it, even though it's in Jeffery's name. Unfortunately, that's not something I could have asked the good doctor, even if I'd known what was going on with his brother."

"Too true, I'm afraid. Well once we get our hands on the scumbag—Peter, I mean—we can ask him."

"And we will. Along with where he's keeping the girls, if they're still alive."

"Not a thought I like."

"Me neither."

Chapter Fourteen

Reaper parked the car a block from the address they had for Peter Kinsley. It was a small, one-story house, approximately twenty blocks from Off-the-Street, in a marginally better area containing lower-middle class homes and occasional shops. Reaper and Wrath were dressed in jeans, blue work shirts and dark jackets — which was a step up from the homeless men they'd been portraying for the last few days.

They strolled casually down the street. Just two men returning from a visit to the local bar three blocks behind them.

As they passed Kinsley's house, Wrath nodded toward the carport. "Looks like he's not home."

"Presumption, but logical," Reaper replied.

They continued down the block to the corner then took a right, walking until they reached the alley that ran behind the house. The streetlight cut the darkness for a few yards, then they were in deep shadows as they made their way to the back of Kinsley's place. They saw a small yard, surrounded by a chest-high slatted wooden fence with no gate. Not that it stopped them from entering the yard, once they ascertained that no one was watching.

"Do we want to check out the house?" Wrath asked.

"As long as we're in the neighborhood," Reaper replied with a small smile.

The windows had either curtains or Venetian blinds on them. The curtains were tightly drawn, but the blinds had seen better days and a few of the slats were bent enough that they could peer into the two rooms behind them. One was a kitchen, which didn't surprise Reaper. The second room appeared to be a bedroom from the dresser he could barely make out at the wall opposite the window. If there was a bed, it was positioned where it wasn't visible. From their locations at the side and front of the house, he figured the curtained windows were for the living and dining rooms.

"He has a basement," Wrath barely murmured, pointing to two low windows beside the back porch. They were uncovered, but there wasn't enough ambient light to see what was inside. There were two more on the right side of the house, under what they presumed was the dining room window. They couldn't see into the basement through them either.

"Either it's a half-basement, or he's blocked off any windows on the other side, Reaper pointed out after checking.

"Meaning there could be a room there where he had the girls when he took those pictures."

Reaper nodded. "I'd like to get inside, but we don't know when he'll be back."

"Assuming he's not inside and asleep," Wrath pointed out. "If the car is his brother's, he may not be able to use it on a daily basis, which would explain why it's not here."

"True, I guess. Still, you'd think he'd need it to get to and from work."

"We passed a bus stop on the way here."

"Good point." Reaper started back to the alley. He was just to the fence when headlights announced a car was coming down the street. Quickly, both men got over the fence, and just in time. A brown car that matched the description of the one they were interested in pulled into the driveway and parked in the carport. The man who got out wore too-tight jeans and a sweatshirt that did nothing to hide his muscular arms.

"That *has* to be him," Wrath whispered, his lips close to Reaper's ear as he peered between two slats in the fence. "Red hair and all."

"Damned good thing we didn't try to get into the house," Reaper murmured, also looking between the slats.

"Definitely," Wrath agreed.

The man vanished from view, going around to the front of the house.

As he and Wrath moved back down the alley, Reaper said, "Now we have a direct connection between Peter Kinsley and the car."

"Yep. So the next step is to put a tracker on it."

"If we had one," Reaper pointed out.

"We will by tomorrow night."

Reaper cocked an eyebrow. "From the station house?"

"Yep."

"Legitimately?"

Wrath chuckled. "Define 'legitimate'."

"Okay, that answers that question."

By then, Reaper and Wrath were at the car. They got in and Reaper drove to the building that would, he hoped — with luck and money — become the new home of Off-the-Street.

"Time for act two," he said, after parking behind it. They took two battered overcoats from the trunk, putting them on after taking off the jackets they were wearing, adding their grungy watchcaps. "Once more, dear friend, into the breach," Reaper muttered.

"I believe it's, once more unto the breach, dear friends," Wrath replied with a grin, earning him a raised middle finger from Reaper.

* * * *

Despite everything else that Zack had been involved with, he'd managed over the past two weeks to put in some time with Mr. Mackie — his client who was on the board of the Gold Hotel — planning the fund raising gala for Off-the-Street's new home. Now Zack, Mackie and Brian were in Zack's office going over the finalized plans. Also there, although as a silent partner, was Kozak.

When Brian entered the office with the dog at his side, Mackie looked at Kozak with interest. Once Brian was seated, his crutches lying on the floor next to the chair, Mackie asked if he could pet Kozak. Brian gave a hand signal, and the greyhound walked to Mackie, pressing against the man's knee while Mackie stroked his head.

"He's very well trained," Mackie commented.

Brian smiled. "He has to be. He goes with me everywhere now, including the shelter."

"How did he lose his leg?"

"The people at the animal shelter didn't know. He was found wandering along the highway close to a rest stop, and a Good Samaritan brought him to them. Since he wasn't chipped, and no one came to claim him, they figure someone had just dropped him off at rest stop before going on their way to who knows where."

"People like that should be shot," Mackie muttered. "He's beautiful." He patted Kozak's head again then pointed at Brian. Much to his and Zack's surprise, the dog immediately went over to his owner, settling down at Brian's feet.

"So where do things stand at this point?" Brian asked

"The Crystal Room is booked for the gala, on Saturday the sixteenth."

"That's in just a little over a week," Brian said with a worried frown. "How come you're just telling me now?"

"Because I know you," Zack told him. "You're fantastic when it comes to running Off-the-Street, but not so much so when it has to do with things outside your area of expertise. Don't worry. We'll be ready. Invitations to the bigwigs, so to speak, are going out this afternoon. And there will be a write-up in the society column in the paper tomorrow, as well as a half-page ad promoting the gala, since it will be open to anyone who can afford a ticket."

"That gives everyone who's coming a chance to shop this week for what they'll be wearing," Mackie added. "Did Zack tell you we're going with an eighties theme? Karaoke, a DJ, a club-like atmosphere, dancing of course."

"With the lights?" Brian asked hopefully. "I remember lights."

"All that and more," Mackie replied with a grin.

Brian frowned again. "Do you...? Will we make enough to cover the hotel's costs and still have something left to buy the building?"

"Brian, by the time the party is over, you'll be able to buy two buildings. I promise," Zack assured him.

"To be honest, I'll believe it when I see it."

Zack took a paper from the file sitting on the table in front of them. He handed it to Brian, saying, "The list of invitees."

Brian looked at it and whistled. "The mayor? The governor? Them?" He tapped a couple of names. "Are you kidding me?"

"Nope. You'd be surprised how many people want to see the shelter find a new home."

"Including the hotel board," Mackie put in. "We took a vote, and the hotel is covering all the costs of the gala."

"Holy shit!" Brian exclaimed. "Sorry. I mean, oh my God."

Mackie chuckled. "Either one works. To be honest, it's good publicity for us, so it was a no-brainer."

"Maybe our dream really will come true," Brian said softly, looking a Zack.

"It's going to, Brian. It *will*."

* * * *

The moment Zack got upstairs, he saw the tracking device they needed sitting on the dresser. "How did you get that when you didn't work today?" he asked Dallas while he hung up his suit coat and took off his dress shirt.

Dallas replied, "Went shopping. I figured it was better to do it that way than take the chance of faking a reason for needing one for the guy at the precinct who handles them. I do, believe it or not, value my job."

"I always knew you were smarter than you sometimes seem," Zack told him, ducking when Dallas took a swipe at him. He backed away quickly when Dallas tried again. "Want to play, huh?"

Dallas smirked. "When don't I?" Since Zack was close to the bed, Dallas tackled him, landing them both on it.

"Damn. Let me at least get out of my shoes and slacks."

"Go for it," Dallas replied, rolling off him.

Zack instantly took advantage of that to wrestle Dallas onto his back and grab his wrists, holding them above Dallas' head with one hand while diving in for a fast kiss.

"That the best you can do?" Dallas asked, looking up at him with a sly grin.

Rather than answering, Zack kissed him again. This time it was slow and passionate when Dallas opened to him. In the intensity of the moment, Zack's hold on Dallas' wrists loosened. With a sudden twist, Dallas freed them, wrapped his arms around Zack, and without breaking the kiss, reversed their positions. Then he pulled back, resting on his elbows. "Now, as I was saying…"

"I should… No, *we* should finish undressing. And I think I was the one who—"

"Shush." Dallas leaned down and they kissed again for a long moment. "Now, we undress," he said, scooting off Zack to the edge of the bed. "First one finished gets to top."

Zack snorted. "You're only wearing… Okay, that was fast." He stood long enough to kick off his shoes and get rid of his slacks, briefs and socks before crawling back on the bed again. He knelt, gripping the railing of the headboard then looked back at Dallas, who was watching him with a lustful gaze. "Well? Are you just going to sit there?"

"Maybe? I like the view from here. It really turns me on."

"Dallas," Zack growled. "I think we were both turned on the minute I came into the room."

"No. First we talked about —"

"Will you quit and fuck me before I have to take care of this" — he grabbed his hard cock in one hand, stroking it — "on my own."

"Can I watch?" Dallas asked, a big grin lighting his face.

"No. Go downstairs and see what's for supper," Zack replied, repressing a grin of his own.

"Not in this lifetime." Dallas got the lube from the nightstand drawer, squirting a liberal dose on his fingers. Putting one hand on Zack's hip, he eased a greased finger through his lover's tight ring of muscle. He touched then stroked Zack's gland, smiling when Zack moaned deeply. "Maybe I'll just do this until you come."

"Fuck no! I want your cock inside me."

"Do you, now?"

"Now would be the operative word in that sentence," Zack managed to get out amidst his intensifying groans.

After using his fingers to stretch Zack, Dallas readied himself with a generous amount of lube before pressing the swollen head of his cock to Zack's waiting hole and easing in.

"I'm not going to break, damn it," Zack said, now gripping the headboard again with both hands. "Not after all these years of us —"

"God, you're talky." Dallas pushed in further but still slowly. Then with one thrust, his cock was fully engulfed. Leaning over, he kissed the nape of Zack's neck, murmuring, "Love you."

"Love you too," Zack replied. "But if you don't move right now, that might change real fast."

Dallas laughed as he began to ride Zack. "Wouldn't…want that."

"Didn't…think…so…" Zack managed to gasp out.

While he thrust in, pulled back and drove in again, Dallas wrapped one hand around Zack's cock, eliciting deep groans from his lover. They moved in well-practiced tandem as pleasure mounted until, with one final push, Dallas arched back and came with a cry of release. Zack's shout of elation followed moments later, as he shook from the strength of his orgasm.

"I'll never…get tired…of making love to you," Dallas whispered, collapsing on Zack's back when Zack dropped onto the bed.

"I second that," Zack replied softly.

A few minutes and several kisses later, Dallas crawled off the bed, telling Zack, "We have time for a quick shower. Then supper, and back to bed to get some sleep." He barely remembered, when they were finally in bed again, to set the alarm for midnight.

* * * *

"We're in luck," Reaper said under his breath when he saw the brown car sitting in Peter Kinsley's carport.

He had parked his own car, the one he rarely used because it was a true beater, a block away. Reaper had bought it when he'd gotten his first job after getting off the streets. It had served him well and he was loath to get rid of it, despite its age. Now he was glad he hadn't. It would fit well in the neighborhoods where they needed to monitor Kinsley's movements. They could stay well away from him by using the tracker Wrath was going to put on Kinsley's car, and still be able to catch up with the man if he tried to grab one of the girls. Something they couldn't do on foot.

"No lights showing," Wrath said, just as softly. "At least, not from here." He stepped out from the shadow of the tree where they were standing then inched his way along the side of the yard to Kinsley's car. Reaper saw him kneel for a moment, reaching under the side of the car not visible from the house.

A minute later, Wrath was back beside Reaper. "Done and done. Now we wait."

When they returned to Reaper's car, Wrath took out his smartphone and brought up the program that would let him follow Kinsley's movements. "We have lift off," he said after about twenty minutes passed.

Staying a block back and one east of Kinsley, Reaper followed Wrath's directions on where the man was heading.

They were well into the area around Off-the-Street when Wrath said, "He's slowing down. Probably cruising to see if he can find a girl he wants."

At the same time, Reaper's cell vibrated. Taking it out, he saw he had a text from Zip.

Brown car, by the schoolyard.

Reaper texted back his thanks and told Wrath, who nodded.

"That's what I'm getting too, but it's still moving."

"If Zip's there, chances are some of the other guys are too, so Kinsley's playing it smart and avoiding a confrontation with them."

"Yep. Turn at the next corner."

"Right or left?" Reaper asked, slowing down.

"Sorry. Left."

Reaper did, and they went three blocks before Wrath told him to pull over and douse the lights. Reaper saw why a moment later when the brown car crossed the intersection ahead of them. Reaper waited then took off, not turning on the headlights as he turned left again. The brown car was a block ahead of them, maintaining a steady twenty miles per hour. Then it went right and slowed down in front of a building.

"He's getting out," Wrath said as they reached the corner.

Reaper didn't stop, but he glanced over to see why Kinsley had. The light from a bulb above an entryway showed him two girls, standing on the steps leading up to the door of the building. Reaper parked out of sight, a few yards beyond the cross street. He and Wrath got out of their car then moved to the shadows of the buildings, inching their way down to the corner.

Peering cautiously around the building, Reaper saw Kinsley, deep in a discussion with the girls. He tensed, ready to move if he tried to grab one of them. Then the man turned slightly and the light above him lit his face. Reaper instantly stepped back. "That," he said very softly to Wrath, "is not Peter Kinsley. In fact it's not any of the Kinsley brothers."

"Then who the hell…?" Wrath paused when they saw him go back to the car, alone. "It's the right car."

They watched as he got into it and drove away.

Wrath checked his phone, with his hands cupping it so the light wouldn't show. "Looks like he's heading back to the house—and taking the most direct route," he said a couple of seconds later.

"Let's talk to the girls." Reaper rounded the corner, walking swiftly to the doorway.

The younger girl eyed him, shaking her head. "Don't think you're getting a freebie, just 'cause you're on the down and out, dude."

Reaper shook his head. "Wouldn't think of asking. I would like to know what the man you were talking to said, however."

"What business is it of yours?" the second girl asked.

Wrath joined them, causing both girls to tense up and back up to the top step. He said, with a slight smile, "Ever hear of Reaper?"

"Yeah, and?"

"Now you can tell your friends you actually met him." Wrath nodded at Reaper.

"Uh-huh. Reaper's big and tough and wear's leathers and for damned sure, he's not him."

Reaper took out his phone, punched in a number, and handed it to her. She looked at it, then him. "What?"

"You know who Zip is?"

"Well, yeah."

"Talk to him. Ask him about me."

Putting the phone to her ear, she said, "Zip? Yeah, it's me, Dani. There's a guy here claims he's Reaper but..." She nodded, looking up at Reaper. "Yeah, I guess. Okay. Thanks." She hung up, giving back the phone. "From what he said, you're Reaper. So, umm..."

"The man you were talking to. What did he want?"

Dani snorted. "Three guesses."

Reaper chuckled. "That I figured. But why did he leave?"

"'Cause the word's out we shouldn't get in any cars with a john, and he wasn't willing to go down to the alley."

"He wasn't a happy camper when we told him no deal," the younger girl told him. "Said he'd pay Dani fifty to blow him while he did me."

"I'd pay to see that. All three of you in the front seat," Wrath muttered.

"It's possible." Dani grinned. "Want us to show you?"

"Umm, I'll pass thanks."

"Okay, question time," Reaper said. "Did you notice anything about him, like jewelry, an accent, anything that would make him stand out if we run into him?"

The younger one shook her head.

Dani started to then frowned. "Yeah. He had a couple of rings. One was gold, wide, with some design on it. On his" — she looked at her hands — "his left hand."

"A wedding band?" Wrath asked.

"Maybe? It was on the right finger. The other one looked like the kind you get when you graduate. Not that I ever did, but I met a guy once. He had a college ring with a stone and the name of the school. The ring this guy wore was like that, with a square red stone maybe the size of my thumbnail, and words around it. I couldn't read them but..." Dani shrugged.

"That's still a big help. Anything else?"

The younger girl chewed her lip. "I think maybe he dyes his hair. It was sorta red but when he was under the light, I could see black roots."

"You're very observant," Reaper told her with a smile.

She blushed, looking down at her feet.

"You both are. Now, if I were you, I'd find somewhere else to hang out, just in case. And if you ever see him again... Do you have phones?"

"I do," Dani replied.

"Good. If you see him, call me." He told her the number to his throwaway, watching her program it into her phone. Then, after thanking the girls again for their help, he and Wrath went back to the car. He made it a point to drive by where the girls had been and was glad to see they must have taken his advice because they were gone.

"If that wasn't Kinsley," Wrath said as they headed back to Kinsley's house, "who the hell was it and why was he driving Kinsley's car?"

"If we knew the answer to that, we'd be well on our way to stopping him. He's obviously got access to the car, whether Kinsley knows it or not."

"So probably a friend or acquaintance of his."

"Somehow I doubt it's a friend, but it has to be someone who knows his habits to know he can use the car without Kinsley being aware that it's gone. Perhaps someone who lives in the neighborhood."

"That's definitely possible, given the fact that our perp tries to grab girls well after midnight." Wrath tapped a fingernail against his teeth. "The Facebook page we found is a fake."

"Unless Kinsley knows what's going on, I'd say that's a given. Why pick him to be the patsy?"

"Maybe I should have a talk with him, but not as Wrath."

Reaper chuckled. "Yeah. Somehow, looking the way you do now, I doubt he'd do more than slam the door in your face."

They were on Kinsley's street now. As they drove by his house, they saw the brown car parked on the carport.

"Let's get back home," Wrath said. "I'll get ready for work then pay Kinsley a visit before I go in."

"At six-thirty in the morning?"

"It might shock him enough he'll be willing to think and talk."

* * * *

Kinsley's car was still on the carport and light shown through the curtains in one of the front windows when

Dallas arrived, so he knew someone was home. He parked, went to the front door and rang the bell. It took a minute before he heard someone unlock the door, then it opened as widely as the chain would allow.

"Officer, can I help you?" the man, presumably Peter Kinsley, asked.

"I have a few questions for you about your car, Mr. Kinsley," Dallas replied.

"My car?" Since he didn't deny he was Kinsley, Dallas knew he had the right man.

"The Chevy Malibu on your carport."

"I..." The man hesitated before closing the door. It opened fully a second later and Kinsley, dressed in a bus driver's uniform stood there. "I'm pretty sure my tags are up to date," he said.

"They are. This has to do with something else. May I come in?"

With obvious reluctance, Kinsley stepped aside. "I have to leave in a few minutes to get to work."

"This shouldn't take long," Dallas told him, entering into the small, very neat living room. He took out his notebook, ostensibly reading something written in it. "We have a report that a car matching the description of yours, down to the license plate, was involved in a possible attempted kidnapping."

Kinsley looked at him in shock. "You have to be kidding me!"

"No, sir. It happened two nights ago. Two young women were approached by a man driving your car. I would say you were the driver, except now that I see you, the description they gave the officers doesn't match. Did you lend the car to someone? A friend or acquaintance?"

"Good Lord. No. No I didn't. I wouldn't because, if you must know, I don't own the car. It belongs to my brother and he's been letting me use it since mine was involved in a bad wreck a couple of months ago." Kinsley grimaced. "Luckily, I wasn't badly hurt, but the car was totaled and I can't afford to buy a new one yet."

"I'm sorry to hear that."

"I have a question," Kinsley said, frowning. "Since it's in my brother's name, how did you track it down to me?"

"We contacted him first. He told us about letting you use it."

"Oh." Kinsley's shoulders slumped. "So now he thinks I'm—what?—out trying to molest young women or something?"

"No, sir," Dallas replied with a smile. "The first thing he said, when he was asked about the car, was that you had it. At that point, the officer who talked to him implied that you had a few unpaid parking tickets and left it at that."

"Thank God. But... How could someone be using it without my knowledge?"

"That's what I'd like to know," Dallas said. "According to the girls, it was around three a.m. when the incident happened. It's possible that whoever the man was stole your car and returned it when he was unsuccessful. "

Kinsley frowned. "I...suppose he could, if he found the spare key I keep in one of those magnetic boxes in the wheel-well."

"Not very smart, since that's one of the first places a thief will check," Dallas said dryly. "I should tell you, this isn't the first time this has happened. Your car has been spotted at least twice before in Uptown. Always very early in the morning. Always where homeless girls...hang out."

"In other words, girls who are selling themselves."

"Yes."

"Well it for damned sure wasn't me driving, but I can't think of anyone I know who would have borrowed the car without asking permission first. Besides which, everyone I know has a car of their own."

"That doesn't negate someone using yours. Do you have any enemies?"

Kinsley snorted. "I'm not the kind of guy who makes enemies. Unless you count someone I had to kick off my bus for causing trouble. I doubt they'd come looking for me to take my car so they can pick up streetwalkers."

"True. What about your neighbors?"

"I don't know them all that well, but doesn't the same thing hold? Why steal my car to do this then return it later?" Kinsley glanced at the clock on the wall over the TV and grimaced. "Can we talk about this tonight? I have to get to work."

Dallas told him that he couldn't use his car for that, since the police would have to go over it for fingerprints. *Or I will, since I'm not here in an official capacity.* "I'll give you a ride to your job, if you like. And I'll need the keys to the car."

With a sigh, Kinsley handed them over. "I hope you find something. Maybe I should just give it back to my brother. After all, I can ride the bus for free when I'm in uniform. I did that for a few days before Jeffery let me borrow the car."

"Unless we find anything other than prints, and we might not find those if the thief is smart enough to wear gloves, you should be able to use it again tonight."

"I'm getting a car alarm," Kinsley stated adamantly. "On my way home. I should have had one to begin with but hell, it's not mine, and not exactly new, so…"

"Under the circumstances, I'm sure the car is exactly what the perp was looking for. Nice, but it doesn't stand out. Why don't you grab what you need and I'll take you to work."

Ten minutes later, Dallas dropped him off at the bus company garage. "Give me your number," he told Kinsley, "and I'll call you as soon as we're finished with the car."

"Thanks." Kinsley blew out a long breath. "I hope you catch whoever it is."

"As do I," Dallas agreed.

* * * *

As soon as he'd dropped Kinsley off at work, Dallas headed in to the station house, making it just in time for roll call. When it was over, he told Mike he'd be a minute, before going to pick up a fingerprint kit. Then he joined him at the car.

"What's that for?" Mike asked as they took off.

"Umm, to lift prints from an object," Dallas replied, straight-faced.

Mike gave him the finger. "I know that, but why do we need one?"

"I ran into a man I know from church," Dallas said, fudging the truth a bit. "He said he thought someone was using his car without authorization, so I told him I'd see if I could get some prints off the steering wheel and run them. Probably won't happen, but I figure it's worth a try."

"Did he report it?"

"No. He said he'd feel stupid if it turned out he was wrong. You know how people are." Dallas gave Mike the address and they headed to Kinsley's house. Taking the kit, Dallas unlocked Kinsley's car then dusted the interior for prints. He found several relatively clear ones and used the lifting tape to capture them, putting the print on the tape onto a white index card. When he was satisfied he'd gotten a fair sample, he returned to the patrol car. "Unless the person borrowing the car is an idiot, these all probably belong to the owner, but it's worth a shot."

Going back to the station, Dallas turned the prints over to one of their technicians to run. He asked her to let him know as soon as she got a hit on any of them, then he and Mike went out on patrol.

* * * *

Zack was at the tail end of a meeting with a client when Alice buzzed him, saying he had a call from Mr. Comstock. He asked her to tell him he'd call in back in ten minutes and finished up with the client.

Then he dialed Dallas' cell and was immediately greeted with, "Can you take a lunch break?"

After checking his schedule, Zack said he could in half an hour and they agreed to meet at a small diner they frequented occasionally, well outside of Uptown.

Zack arrived to find Dallas already had a booth at the back. "What did you do with Mike?" Zack asked as he slid in opposite Dallas.

"Told him I had a heavy lunch date with a guy I met at a club. He snickered, dropped me off and went home to eat lunch with his wife. He's picking me up in half an hour." Dallas hesitated, looking at the menu, even though Zack knew he had it memorized.

"What do you not want to tell me?" Zack asked with a small smile.

"I got prints off of Kinsley's car and had them run. Most of them, of course, are his. But we got a hit on one that wasn't. I called him to ask if he knew the man they belonged to. He said he didn't." He looked worriedly at Zack. "Okay, don't shoot me, but I told Kinsley to file a report that his car was being used without his authorization."

Zack nodded slowly, glad when the waitress appeared just then to take their orders. He needed time to process Dallas' information. He wasn't happy about it. Not that they knew who had been using the car, but the fact that, if he was right, the police would be on the case now. He had sort of known it was inevitable, but still... *It's my job to keep the kids safe.* He sighed, and when the waitress left, he asked, "Who did the print belong to?"

"A known felon with a rap sheet a mile long. Mostly for loitering with intent to pick up a female for sexual purposes. Not too long ago, a girl filed a report on him, saying he tried to force her into his car. But his lawyer got him off on that one because she was a user as well as having been picked up a couple of times for propositioning men."

"So now it's out of our hands," Zack said.

"Yeah. I get that you wanted to deal with this guy, but damn it, Zack, I'm a cop first, like it or not. We have the resources to find him and deal with him legally."

"I know." Zack reached across the table to take his hand, smiling. "There's nothing wrong with being a cop. One of my best friends is and I like him anyway. To be honest, I knew this would probably happen sooner or later, once you decided to spend part of your time on the dark side."

Dallas waited until the waitress had set down their meals and left before replying.

"It's not really the dark side. Just a deep shade of gray. I have no problem dealing with the punks who go after the homeless with intent to harm them. But this is more than that, if we're right."

"How is Kinsley going to explain he thinks someone is using his car and the let the police know he's afraid it's for something illegal?" Zack asked after taking a bite of his sandwich.

"He'll tell whoever he talks to that as far as he can figure, the thief found the spare key in the wheel-well and uses the car sometime between when he goes to bed, and morning, since the car is always there when he gets up. He's going to say that he only suspected something because he noticed added mileage and that he's needed to fill up more often than normal. He's just sure it's some kid joyriding, but he wants it stopped. I also asked him to say he got in contact with me because we knew each other from church and he knows I'm a cop."

Zack snorted. "You haven't seen the inside of a church since forever."

Dallas grinned. "No one has to know that but you and me, and it works. Better than saying I met him at the grocery store, which was my first idea."

"Yeah, true."

They continued eating, remaining silent for a while.

Then Zack said, "You're sure he doesn't know the guy the fingerprint belongs to?"

"So he says. Short of giving him a lie detector test, there's really no way to prove differently. I'm sure he'll be grilled up and down about it, though."

"One would hope so. Is there any way to give the description of the man Dani and the others have seen to whoever gets Kinsley's case?"

"Not that I can think of, but, I do have an admitting photo of the guy from his last arrest. We can show it to the kids just to be certain Willie Howarth is the man they saw."

Zack snickered. "Willie?"

"Yeah. Fits sort of. Anyway, when we're out tonight, we'll show the photo around to see if any of the girls recognize him."

"What about staking out Kinsley's car?"

"That will be done, I'm sure. Unfortunately, at this point, I'm out of it. At least officially."

"Unofficially, if we see him, we're not going to make an anonymous call to nine-one-one," Zack said, scowling.

"We should call, but yeah, maybe we deal out a little hurt first, just so he learns his lesson."

"That works. And I think your ride is here," Zack told him, seeing a patrol car pull up in front of the diner. "I'll see you when you get home."

Dallas nodded, murmuring, "Love you," as he got up.

"You sticking me with the tab?" Zack asked with a grin.

"Damned straight. You make twice what I do."

Chuckling, Zack said, "Love you too," then watched as Dallas hurried out of the diner to get in the car.

Chapter Fifteen

Thanks to the fingerprint Dallas had found in Kinsley's car, and good police work, Willie Howarth was picked up two days later, soon after he arrived at Kinsley's house around two a.m. and tried to take the car again. He ran when he realized the police were closing in on him, making it back to his home three blocks away. When they stopped him from leaving in his own car, the officers confiscated a bag he was just tossing into the trunk. It contained photos of underage girls.

"Much like the ones I found on Facebook," Dallas told Zack that evening.

Howarth was now in custody for grand theft auto and child pornography.

"They got a warrant, based on the photos, to search his house and found a room in the basement that matches the one in the pictures. There were also addresses on his computer in a well-secured file, not that that stopped our computer expert from finding them. Two of them were for houses out of state belonging to known madams. The police in those districts will check to see if any of the girls in the photos are there."

"We did a good job," Zack said then added wryly, "even if we didn't get to finish it the way we wanted to."

"But it is over and he's going away for a long time — God and the courts willing," Dallas replied, giving Zack a quick hug before stripping off his uniform and going to shower.

He came back into the bedroom a few minutes later, put on a pair of jeans and went in search of Zack and dinner. He found Zack sitting at the kitchen table, a plate of food in front of him, looking a one of the papers from a pile by his elbow. There was a second plate, laden with pot roast and vegetables, at Dallas' place, so he sat, picking up one of the papers as he began to eat. "This is going to be quite an extravaganza," he commented.

"I know," Zack agreed. "Thankfully it's all being handled by the hotel's party planner now, as far as pulling it together. Mr. Mackie gave me these so I could take one final look, especially at the guest list — in case we missed someone who should be on it. Brian has the same list." Zack chuckled. "I think Brian's feeling very overwhelmed right now. He called me to ask if we couldn't postpone it for a week — or a year."

"It's a bit late for that, isn't it? Considering it's happening this Saturday."

"He was kidding — mostly. I got him calmed down. He said before calling me he'd talked to Mackie to give him a couple more names." After putting the paper back on the pile, Zack took a couple of bites of roast before saying, "Will you come with me?"

It was a logical question. They rarely, if ever, went out in public together. Dallas was out, but given that he was a cop, he didn't flaunt his sexuality. For Zack, it had never really come up as he had few friends outside of Brian, given that he'd spent the last few years of his life moving between his real job and the one he'd taken on as a protector of the homeless.

Putting down his utensils, Dallas looked at Zack, his lips quirking up. "It would be a hell of a way to announce we're a couple."

"But you're willing to?"

"Yeah, I am. Hell, Mike keeps pushing me to hit up the clubs and find someone. Now I can get him off my back."

"He what?" Zack looked at him in dismay.

"Whenever I get stressed, that's his idea of a cure. And I did — once. Met a really great man." He grinned at Zack. "One whom I wouldn't trade for the world. So, yes, we'll go to this shindig together."

"You do realize you'll have to rent a tux."

"Ugh. Maybe I'll reconsider."

"Nope." Zack leaned over to kiss him. "You said yes. No take-backs."

Dallas snorted. "That was childish."

"You keep me feeling young, so it was warranted."

"Uh-huh. Try again."

"Kissing you? Gladly." He cupped one hand behind Dallas' head, kissing him deeply.

Dallas returned it quite heartily before saying, "We'd better finish supper and get to bed. We have to be up again in six hours and counting."

"Taskmaster," Zack grumbled.

"It's not my fault you decided to save the world — or at least a small part of it."

"And it happens more often, now that I have company."

"Always and forever, in every way," Dallas replied softly. "Now...eat."

* * * *

"It should have been you, not the damn cops, who took care of that bastard," Raven said, glaring at Reaper.

Next to her, China and Zip nodded in agreement.

"I agree. But it would only have been a temporary fix. He'd have been back before you know it," Reaper replied. "This way, he'll end up in jail for a good long time, and that's partly because of the help we got from all of you in tracking him down."

Zip grinned. "We done good with that."

"You did well," Wrath said.

"Now you're an English teacher?" Zip shook his head. "What are you guys? I mean, in real life."

"This *is* real life, Zip," Wrath told him. "We're just two men, who want to make it better for you, if we can."

"You're doing okay with that," China said. "And pretty soon, maybe Off-the-Street is going to be better too."

Reaper nodded. "No maybe about it. It definitely will be."

"Still didn't answer my question."

Zip studied Wrath, who was, as always, dressed like a homeless man. This time he wore a tattered jacket over a gray hoodie with the hood pulled up. "I know you from somewhere," Zip said. "Just can't figure out where."

"Bet he's a cop," Raven told him with a laugh. "Or maybe a social worker." Turning serious, she added,

"Those are the only people we ever meet face-to-face who actually see who we are and give a damn about getting us off the streets."

"What about Brian?" Reaper asked.

"Him too, though he's *sort* of a social worker. Just not in a fancy office. I wish…"

When Raven didn't continue, Reaper asked, "What do you wish?"

"That there was some way we could help too."

"Tell you what," Reaper said. "Why don't I talk to Brian? Maybe—once the shelter has moved into the new building—he'll have some ideas about what you—all of you—can do. Like an outreach program. I know he's talked about that a couple of times."

"Really? Damn. I could get down with that," Zip said. "Well, as long as I don't have to preach to the kids. Not doing that 'cause it's a big turn-off. At least, for me it is."

"Me too," China agreed.

Reaper chuckled. "Has Brian ever done that to you all?"

"Well…no," Zip admitted.

"Then I doubt he'd want you to do it when you're handing out food and condoms."

"Yeah, good point, I guess."

"So I'll let him know you guys might be interested, if he starts one. For now, though, Wrath and I have to get moving."

"Yeah, we know. Keeping the world safe for democracy."

Wrath laughed, glancing at Reaper. "Not quite, but at least trying to keep your world safe."

"You are!" China said, suddenly hugging Reaper. "Both of you are. Thank you!"

"No thanks needed," Reaper replied quietly, hugging her back. "Now off with you, and find somewhere safe to crash. I don't want to be saving your asses if I don't have to." He smiled when Zip saluted before the trio took off.

"They're good kids," Wrath said as he and Reaper headed in the opposite direction.

"Most of them are," Reaper agreed. "Despite what they've been through, most of them are."

Chapter Sixteen

"You look very handsome," Zack said, as he adjusted Dallas' bowtie.

"I feel like a damn penguin." To demonstrate, Dallas waddled across the bedroom, much to Zack's amusement.

"That doesn't negate the handsomeness, so collect your wallet and keys and let's get a move on. We don't want to be late."

Dallas gathered his things, saying, "I thought being late was fashionable."

"Let's leave that to the bigwigs. I think Brian would appreciate us being there on time to give him some moral support."

A little over half an hour later, they walked into the Crystal Room of the Gold Hotel.

"Boy, this takes me back," Dallas murmured, looking around.

"You were what—all of three in 1985? You can't remember what it was like back then."

"Movies, my dear man. Lots of bad eighties movies I watched with my dad."

"I remember that. Well not on a bar, but the game," Zack said almost wistfully, looking at the Pac-Man figures decorating the bar along one wall. "And fluorescent pink and blue lights."

"Like you were old enough to get into clubs back then."

"Wasn't, but I snuck into one." Zack laughed. "And got kicked out two minutes later, but I still got a look at the lights."

"What do you think?" Mr. Mackie asked, coming up beside Zack.

"You did a great job. It looks like people are getting into the theme," Zack replied, watching a few couples already out on the dance floor at one end of the room. "No disco ball?"

Mackie laughed. "That is *so* last year, or more to the point, something from the seventies, as I discovered to my shame, when I suggested it to our party planner. You should stake a claim on a table if you plan on eating. You and…" He looked at Dallas.

"Dallas Comstock," Dallas replied before Zack could.

"A business partner?"

"No," Zack said, putting his arm around Dallas' shoulders. "My life partner."

"Well… I'll be damned. Who knew? Somehow, for whatever reason, I had you pegged as a confirmed bachelor, Zack."

Zack chuckled. "It's been a while since I was." He glanced around. "Is Brian here yet?"

"He is. And he brought a few special guests. I think they're in the game room at the moment."

"The what?"

"We set up a video arcade. After all, this is supposed to be the eighties. It's over there." Mackie pointed to an archway off to their left.

Grinning, Zack said, "This I have to see. And yes, Dallas, those I do remember. They were a great escape from…things. Before I decided to escape for good."

Dallas gave him a tight, if fast, hug, asking, "Is this bringing back bad memories?"

"Not at all. What's past is past and now I have good memories — thanks to you."

By then they were walking through the archway into what was an excellent reproduction of an arcade. There were a few early arrivals huddling over the games at one side of the room.

"Oh, boy," Zack whispered.

Brian sat on padded bench between two of the machines. Several kids in their mid to late teens surrounded one of the boys, cheering him on as he played Gauntlet. The girls were wearing skirts and blouses while the boys had on nice jeans and shirts. If Zack had to guess, they were Brian's special guests. Kids who used the shelter whenever possible.

Which for damned sure is fitting, but…

Grinning, the boy playing the game turned to look at one of his friends. It was Zip. Colly was right beside him, and Raven and China stood on the other side, along with a few kids Zack vaguely recognized, although he couldn't put names to the faces.

At the same time that Zack saw the kids, Brian spotted him and Dallas and beckoned them over.

"This could be interesting, to put it mildly," Dallas said.

"No kidding. Why the hell didn't someone warn us?"

"Why would they? No one knows our…" Dallas smiled wryly. "Our secret identities."

"True," Zack agreed as he sat next to Brian. "So what do you think?" Zack asked him, echoing Mackie's question from a few moments ago.

"Takes me back to my childhood," Brian replied. "Or my young adulthood."

"Same with Zack," Dallas said. He stood next to Zack with his back to the kids, obviously trying to act as a shield so the teens wouldn't get a good look at them. "Not me so much. As Zack pointed out, I was only three."

"Brian, look!" Zip called out. "I beat the level. You said I couldn't, but I did."

"So go on to the next one," Brian said, giving Zip a thumbs-up.

"I'm going to try that one," Raven said, heading to the game on the other side of the bench. Suddenly she stopped, looking a Zack. "Uh-uh. No way," she whispered in disbelief.

"Jig's up," Zack said with a small smile, putting a finger to his lips. "But you have to keep it to yourself."

"Keep what to herself?" China asked, joining them. "Oh, my God." She glanced at Dallas, shaking her head. "I...you... Both of you... You're here."

"Shush," Raven told her.

"What's going on?" Brian asked with a puzzled frown.

Zack sighed. "Let's find a quiet room, if we can, and I'll tell you. Raven, if you'd grab Zip and the others. *Please.*"

"Hang on while I see if there's an empty room we can use," Dallas said then strode to a door half hidden from view by one of the machines. He was back moments later, saying, "We're good."

Zack helped Brian to his feet, before handing him his crutches. By then Raven had rounded up the other teens and they all made their way to a small, and at the moment empty, lounge. Once everyone was inside, Dallas closed the door and leaned against it.

As the girls had earlier, Zip looked from Dallas to Zack and back to Dallas again. "Raven was right the other night. You *are* a cop," he said accusingly. "I've seen you patrolling Uptown."

"That's my — what did you call it? — my real-life job," Dallas agreed.

"Okay, does someone want to fill me in on things?" Brian asked.

"You might want to sit first," Zack told him.

"That bad, huh?" Brian took a seat in one of the armchairs. "Okay, lay it on me."

"You've heard of Reaper. Right?" Zack said.

"Hell, everyone in Uptown has. Well, at least all the kids, to hear them tell it. He's a… Well, some would call him a vigilante. I think he's an unsung hero, if the stories going around about him are…" Brian stopped dead, looking up at Zack. "Oh, shit. You?"

Zack shrugged. "In the flesh. And thanks to Zip and company, now you know."

"Fuck, Zack, you coulda told me a long time ago."

"If I had, you'd have tried to talk me out of it, knowing you. What I do — what Reaper does — is necessary, to my way of thinking. But I figured the way I go about it probably wouldn't sit well with you."

"But it's the only way he can do it," Raven said with a hard nod, getting equally firm nods from the others.

"You knew about this, I presume?" Brian said, giving Dallas an exasperated look.

Zip snickered. "Hell, Brian, he's Wrath. Robin to Reaper's Batman."

"You did *not* just go there," Dallas grumbled, earning laughs from the others.

"Kato and Green Hornet?" Colly suggested.

"Butch Cassidy and Sundance," one of the others threw out.

"Do I look like a cowboy?" Dallas asked.

"No." Zip grinned. "You look like a penguin."

Zack bit his lip to keep from laughing before turning serious. "This has to be kept between us." He looked at each teen, one by one. "Otherwise, we won't be able to keep on helping you. At least not the way we have been. That's especially true where Dallas is concerned. He could lose his job."

"Worse than that," Brian said pointedly, "they could end up in prison."

"Shit," Zip muttered. "Truth?"

Zack nodded. "We're not exactly law-abiding. But then neither are the sons of bitches we deal with. Unfortunately, the courts won't take that into consideration when it comes down to it. Vigilantes are not looked on fondly by law enforcement."

"But you're just doing what the cops can't," Raven protested.

"Speaking as one," Dallas told her, "that really doesn't count in the grand scheme of things. Cops might wish they could do what we're doing. Hell, they do sometimes when they…we see the results of some kid being beaten up or raped or worse because they have no safe place to go. Unfortunately, we have to abide by the law. Arrest the perp if we can then more often than not, watch them lawyer up and walk free."

"That's why you're helping Reaper," China said, looking gratefully at Dallas.

"Yep. Pretty much."

"Bet there's another reason too," Colly said. "You and him are like me and Zip. Right?"

"A bit older, a bit wiser, but yeah," Zack replied with a wink.

"That's too cool."

"I think so. Okay, we should get back to the party. After all, it really is for all of you and every other kid who needs Off-the-Street. Just remember…"

"Our lips are sealed," Raven told him before he could finish. "We're not stupid and we need you—both of you."

Zip nodded, looking at Zack. "You never told us what you do in real life."

"What the hell, since you know who I am now, there's no reason not to. I'm an investment counselor." He had the feeling none of the kids really knew what that was, but Zip had asked, so he tried to explain it in a way they'd understand.

"He's also the man who thought up this whole gala to raise money so we could move," Brian said as he stood. "And he found the new building."

"Whoa." Colly looked impressed. "I want to be like you when I grow up."

"Then get off the streets. All of you. If I could do it, you can too," Zack told him.

"Sure gonna try," Raven replied.

"That's all anyone can ask of you."

Chapter Seventeen

Zack woke Sunday morning to the sound of the phone. Groaning, he rolled over to grab it before it woke Dallas as well.

"Zack" — he yawned — "here."

"Did I wake you?"

"Brian? Why are you up at such an ungodly hour?"

Brian chuckled. "Check the time. It's almost noon."

"Okay. That still doesn't answer the question."

"I wanted to thank you again for all you did for the shelter. I just got off the phone with Mr. Mackie. He told me that he had the initial figures on what the gala brought in." Brian paused before saying in apparent disbelief. "We can buy the building, Zack! And fix it up, and furnish it, and… I still can't believe it."

"Oh, ye of little faith. I told you that would happen." Zack was grinning by then, both at Brian's elation and the fact the Dallas was leaning on his shoulder, trying to listen in on the conversation.

"Now I have to get in touch with the man who's selling it, and my lawyer, and hire plumbers and electricians and — shit. I have a list of mile long of things to do," Brian rattled off.

"Take a deep breath and relax. You don't have to figure everything out right this second."

"I bet there are a lot of kids who'd dive in to help fix the place up," Dallas said.

Brian chuckled. "You eavesdropping, Dallas?"

"Well, duh."

"He's right, Brian," Zack said. "We already talked about that. Once the basic work is done to bring the building up to code, put out the word and half the homeless kids in Uptown will descend to help."

"I know. It seems a bit overwhelming right now, but it'll all come together, thanks to you and all the people who donated to the cause."

"Six months from now, you can have a grand opening party to thank them."

Zack could visualize the grin on Brian's face when the man replied, "With you as the guest of honor."

"I'll pass."

They talked for a few more minutes before hanging up. As soon as Zack put the phone back on the charger, he found himself wrapped in a tight embrace.

"You are," Dallas told him, "an exceptional man."

"What brought that on?"

"As if you didn't know." Dallas planted a kiss on Zack's lips. "You take on people's problems and do everything in your power to eliminate them."

"I'm just helping out," Zack protested. "The same as a lot of other people."

"Shush. You're one in a million." Dallas kissed him again. "And I'm going to show you how special you are."

"Any chance I can go to the bathroom first? My bladder is about to burst."

Dallas snorted. "Special and practical. Go. I'm right behind you. Well, not literally, but…"

They were back in bed moments later. Zack was flat on his back with Dallas sprawled over him.

"You are not to move," Dallas told him before kissing him deeply. When the kiss ended, as it had to so they could catch their breaths, Dallas slid down, laving his tongue over Zack's nipples.

Zack groaned when spikes of electricity seemed to travel from there straight to his groin. His groans deepened as Dallas worked his way slowly down, kissing and licking as he went. When he cupped Zack's balls in his hand, rolling them gently, Zack hissed in a breath, his cock growing even harder.

"Now what to do with you," Dallas said with a wicked grin, looking up at his lover.

"If you don't know after all these years, I'm trading you in for a newer model," Zack replied with a gasped laugh.

Dallas proved that he did know. Taking Zack's cock into his mouth, he sucked, licked and swallowed, his fingers tightly wrapped around the base to keep Zack from coming.

"You are…driving me to…distraction," Zack managed to get out, his fingers tangled in Dallas' hair. Then he came when Dallas released his hold on his cock, arching up as his orgasm flooded him.

Dallas pulled back, licking the last traces of cum from Zack's cock. Crawling back up Zack's body, he kissed him, and Zack could taste himself on Dallas' tongue and lips.

"Now it's your turn," Zack said once the kiss was finished. He slid his hand between them, gripping Dallas' hard member. "On your back."

Dallas complied, obviously expecting Zack to go down on him. Zack had other plans, however. Getting the lube, he squirted some onto his fingers then straddled Dallas. Using two fingers, he readied himself, smiling when he saw Dallas watching lustfully. Soon, he withdrew his fingers and liberally lubed Dallas' rampant, leaking member. "Ready?"

"Oh, yeah. More than, and you know it."

Zack eased down on Dallas' cock, all the time watching his lover's face, loving the heated expression he was engendering. When he was fully settled, Zack leaned in to kiss the man he loved with all his heart. Dallas' passion as he responded to the kiss told Zack he was loved in return.

Then, slowly at first, Zack rode Dallas, the pleasure he was giving him returned when Dallas stroked him until his cock was hard again. Soon they were moving with well-practiced ease, ecstasy mounting until as one they exploded with matching cries of release.

"Thank you," Dallas whispered long moments later.

"For making love to you?" Zack asked with a broad smile.

"No. For loving me."

"How could I help but love you? You are the man who makes life worth living."

"Back at you," Dallas replied, gripping Zack's shoulders to ease him down for a heartfelt kiss. "Now, I suppose, we should get up, as much as I hate the idea."

"Probably. I worked up an appetite and I don't think lunch is going to come upstairs to us."

"Well, damn," Dallas said, giving an exaggerated pout.

Laughing, Zack kissed him again then disentangled himself and slid off the bed to go shower. Dallas joined him, and they managed to wash without engaging in another bout of sex. *Not that we have it in us at the moment for that to happen.* Zack smiled, knowing they were both well sated, and happily so.

Once they were dressed, Zack led the way downstairs to fix lunch then suggested they go out to the backyard. "So we can enjoy what might be the last half-way warm day before late autumn descends in full force."

* * * *

"One thing about this time of year," Reaper said, gripping his battered overcoat tighter around him, "there are fewer punks out looking to cause trouble."

"But when they do, they do it in spades," Wrath replied, his voice barely above a whisper as he pointed to the alley across from them.

In the dim moonlight, it took Reaper a moment to see what he meant. Then he was following Wrath, racing into the alley right at his heels.

Three young men, who looked barely out of their teens, stood over two homeless people—an older man and his young companion. The pair cowered as the men kicked them with heavy boots.

"Scum like you," one of the attackers growled out, "should be castrated then tossed in the trash like the detritus you are."

"Very descriptive," Reaper said, closing in on the men. "I'm surprised a punk like you even knows what those words mean."

"Well, look who showed up to make our night even more fun. These pieces of garbage"—the assailant spat on his victims—"have friends. Come on. Show us what you got," he said, whipping out a switchblade and flicking it open.

The other two attackers, though weaponless, looked ready to back up their leader, balling up their gloved hands into fists.

"Three on two. Not bad odds," Wrath commented as he circled to one side of the men, drawing the attention of the two unarmed ones to him.

One of them took a swing, only to find himself on the ground when Wrath grabbed his arm, twisted and kicked his knee in one fluid motion.

Reaper danced away from the thrusts of the knife blade, glancing between it and the punk's face, looking for tells as to his next move.

The punk sneered, taunting Reaper. "Afraid of a little knife?" He lashed out, ducking then jumping back when Reaper made a grab for him. "You can do better than that, you filthy piece of trash."

"I believe that would be you," Reaper replied as he shook his arm. The knife he had concealed in his sleeve appeared in his hand and he lunged forward. If it hadn't been for a patch of ice beside a Dumpster, he would have slashed the man's arm. Instead, he started to fall and grabbed the edge of the Dumpster to keep from landing on his ass. The punk took a stab at Reaper's hand, leaving a bloody gash across the back of it, before someone twisted the punk's arm behind him. With a shout of rage, he spun halfway around, stabbing at whoever had snagged his wrist. The homeless teen who had been the target of his assault jumped back against the wall next to his companion.

By then, Reaper was in motion again. Coming up behind the attacker, he wrapped his arm around the man's neck and pushed the blade of his knife into his side. "Drop your weapon, or else," he growled.

"Make—" The man never got to finish his sentence. Reaper tightened his chokehold until the man went limp. Dropping him to the ground, Reaper turned to see how Wrath was doing.

Wrath had managed to subdue one of the punks, but apparently, in the process he'd given the other one a chance to grab a stick from somewhere. Now Wrath was backed up against the alley wall, blood flowing from a wound on his forehead. He dodged one blow, only to have a telling one land on his bicep. He hissed in a cry of pain, but managed to avoid being hit again as he kicked out, aiming for his attacker's groin. He missed, his boot landing on the man's thigh instead. That only seemed to enrage Wrath's attacker further. He lunged toward Wrath, using the stick like a sword.

"Some people ain't got no couth," Reaper muttered, snagging the stick, pulling it free of the man's grip. Then he used it effectively to knock the man out cold.

With all of the attackers down for the count, Reaper turned his attention to Wrath, who had slid down the wall onto his ass. "Nasty cut you have there," Reaper told him, taking the small first-aid kit he always carried with him from his coat pocket. "Hold still and let me see."

By then the teen and his companion had joined them. The old man asked, "You want we should tie them up?"

"It might help," Reaper replied while wiping away the blood on Wrath's brow. When the wound was clean, Reaper said, "I think you'll live."

"But will you?" Wrath asked, looking at Reaper's hand. "Seems like you took some damage yourself."

Reaper was surprised to see he was bleeding profusely. "Hope the punk's blade was clean," he grumbled.

The teen came back, kneeling beside them. "Let me see," he said. When Reaper held out his hand, the kid nodded before tearing open a packet holding an antiseptic wipe that he took from the first-aid kit. "This might hurt," he said with a ghost of a smile. "That's what my ma used to tell me when I'd cut myself." He gently cleaned the cut then covered it with a piece of gauze, using two Band-Aids to secure it. "Now you," he said, turning his attention to Wrath. He dealt with Wrath's wound the same way he had Reaper's then sat back on his heels, grinning. "Now I can say I doctored up the two baddest asses in Uptown."

Reaper snorted. "There goes our reputation."

"Not even," the kid replied. "We're gonna tell everyone how the two of you saved our lives."

"For which we greatly thank you," his companion added. "Are you going to call the cops to pick up those punks?"

Wrath glanced at Reaper and chuckled. "After we put them where they belong." He thumbed at the Dumpster.

"Woot," the kid exclaimed, pumping his fist. "Can we help?"

"You bet," Reaper told him.

Five minutes later, the attackers were safely in the Dumpster with the cover down.

"Okay," Reaper said taking out his throwaway. "I suggest the two of you pull a vanishing act before the cops show up."

"We're out of here," the old man replied fervently. "And thanks again."

Reaper made the call, telling the nine-one-one operator where to find the attackers and why they were there. Then he suggested to Wrath that they pay a visit to the local clinic to get their wounds checked. Being a smart man, and wise to what could happen if they didn't, Wrath had no problem with that.

Chapter Eighteen

For the next week, Zack and Dallas took things slowly, letting the damage they'd suffered heal. Mike teased Dallas the day after the fight, suggesting he should stay out of the clubs if he couldn't hold his liquor well enough not to fall on his face. "Or, find a man who'll catch you when that happens," he added with a leer.

Dallas decided, since everyone who had been at the gala now knew about Zack, it was time to let Mike in on the not-so-secret secret. "He does catch me," he replied with a grin. "He catches me when I come home from work, and when we get up in the morning and, well, you get the picture."

"Okay. You're trying to tell me something," Mike said, one eyebrow cocked in question. "Like, you've finally found someone?"

"More like I've had someone for a long time now, but we were keeping quiet about it."

"And you couldn't tell me? Your partner? The man you spend half your time with? I think I should be hurt."

"Sorry. It's…complicated."

"Why?"

"We're not living in the city proper."

"Ah. I see." Which he undoubtedly did, since officers were required to live within the city boundaries.

"I have an address here, you know that, and it's legit. I just… When I first moved in with him, I wasn't willing to take the chance someone would find out I was living there and not here, so keeping quiet about it became a habit."

"Okay. I get it, but you don't have to announce to the world you're living together. Just tell everyone that you and this man are exclusive, and leave it at that."

"That's what I'm thinking. I'm tired of keeping us a secret."

"And how does he feel about it? Will it affect his job?"

"Actually, not at all. You know the gala for the new shelter?"

"Yeah. I almost bought tickets to it, but with Carol due any time now, I decided it wasn't such a great idea. What's the gala got to do with anything, though?"

"He—Zack's his name—was responsible for pulling the whole thing together."

"So the two of you went to it as a couple?"

"Got it in one. And no one seemed to give a damn that he was with me and not some woman."

"Wasn't the chief there?"

Dallas nodded. "He was… Well, surprised is the best word for it. Not that he doesn't know about me, but I don't think he expected me to attend—especially with someone like Zack."

Mike tapped his fingers on the steering wheel then glanced at Dallas. "Would this Zack be Zack Ward?"

"Yep."

"You're flying in good company then. He's one of the movers-and-shakers, even if he does have a reputation for being very reclusive." Mike chortled. "And now I know why."

Not really, but what you're thinking works. Dallas didn't voice that thought, just nodded with a sly grin. "That would about cover it."

"I'm glad you told me, except..."

"Umm?"

"Now I won't be able to rag on you about finding a man to help you relieve your stress."

Dallas laughed. "Sorry. But I'm sure you'll find something else to tease about, knowing you."

"Oh you can bet on that."

* * * *

Zack and Dallas followed Brian into the ground floor of the building Brian now owned, lock, stock and barrel. All the paperwork had been completed to finalize the sale, building permits had been obtained and contractors had already begun work.

"Bet that was the first thing you had the carpenters fix," Zack said, pointing to the new flight of stairs leading to the second floor.

"Yep," Brian agreed. "That and having the elevator brought up to code. That cost a pretty penny, but it was necessary since I seem to be spending more time in the wheelchair than on these." He waved a crutch. "Today is one of my good days."

Zack patted his shoulder, knowing he wasn't looking for sympathy, just stating a fact. "How soon will things be finished enough for the kids to start doing a real cleaning then painting?"

"The electricians are finished. The plumbing for the kitchen and bathrooms will be complete by tomorrow, according to the supervisor. The carpenters are working on the third floor now. When their work is done, we'll have ten rooms up there, plus the two baths. I figure if we use bunk beds again, as we have now, we'll be able to sleep forty kids up there, and another twenty on the second floor. I'm turning the biggest area on the second floor into a classroom and having them break the other two on the same side of the hall into accommodations for the counselors. The bathrooms are ready to use, other than needing to be cleaned and painted, as are the ones on the third floor."

"Sounds great to me," Zack told him.

"What's going in down here?" Dallas asked.

"As you can see, they're in the process of dividing the front space into two parts with an archway between them. The smaller one will be for admitting and the other will be used for distribution of clothes, sleeping bags and such that we give the kids who need them."

"Is there going to be a recreation area?"

"You bet. And a full kitchen-dining room. Come on, I'll show you."

Brian took them into what had been one of the two large rear rooms on the ground floor. It was now an open space that was being shortened by a wall two-thirds of the way in that, at the moment, was just framework.

"There will be two counseling rooms back there, as well as one for the nurse. The rest of this will have sofas, bookshelves, a TV and what have you," Brian explained before going through one of the doorways on the side wall into another large room. At the rear of it, there was a kitchen with a long serving counter, although there were no appliances. When Dallas asked about that, Brian told him they'd bring over the ones from the old Off-the-Street.

"Have you planned how you're getting everything over here?" Zack asked.

Brian nodded. "I found a moving company that can do it all in one day. That way it'll only be a couple of days between when we close the old building and open this one."

"Are you doing anything with the basement?"

"Yep. Thanks to one of the shelter's donors, I'm getting industrial washers and dryers, not the home type we have now. The lockers for the kids who want to leave some of their possessions here will be down there as well, and the rest will be storage for the shelter itself."

"You could also turn a small area into a workshop," Zack suggested. "Use it for classes in wood and metal working."

"I remember those from high school," Dallas said. "I ended up making Mom a nice jewelry box. She still…" He paused suddenly, looking at Zack. "I'll have to take you out there sometime soon to show it to you."

Brian chuckled. "Is that your subtle way of saying you want Zack to meet your family after all these years?"

"Yeah, I guess it is," Dallas replied, still watching Zack as if to gauge his reaction.

"It's about time," Zack said, giving him a hug. "I was beginning to wonder if you sprang fully formed from a cabbage leaf."

Dallas laughed. "You know damn well I didn't."

"I know. Maybe we can plan a trip to visit them after the grand opening here."

"I'd like that."

"Then it's a go. And speaking of going, we'd better head home and get some sleep."

"I'll give you a call as soon as the place is ready for the kids to get to work," Brian said. "I have several older guys and girls, who've already volunteered, but if you run into any more on your...excursions, send them my way. Okay?"

"You bet," Zack told him. "The more the merrier."

Chapter Nineteen

"This may not be a good night," Wrath muttered, a week after their meeting with Brian at the future home of Off-the-Street.

Reaper had the distinct feeling he was correct.

They were inside a one-story, abandoned warehouse in Uptown, looking for Raven and Zip, who were supposedly hanging out there with a couple of friends. The interior walls were covered with graffiti. A couple of dirty mattresses lay in far corner of the rubble-strewn floor. The only light came through a few filthy windows along the street-side wall.

Raven, Zip and their friends weren't there. In fact, when Reaper and Wrath first entered through the unlocked rear door, they were the only humans in the building.

They were halfway down the room, intending to check what they figured had been an office at the front of the building, when the door behind them slammed open. Spinning around, they saw five figures standing there. The men, or teens—it was hard to tell which in the dim light—held weapons such as bats and pipes. One even had what looked like a golf club.

"See, told you we'd get lucky," the tallest of the males said.

"Yeah, Mike," one of the others said.

"Shut your yap, Johnny. No names," Mike said angrily.

"But you just…" Johnny shut up.

"Define 'lucky'," Reaper called out. He pulled back the ragged coat he wore to get his knife from the sheath at his waist.

"Finding two bums who need to be gotten rid of—maybe permanently." As Mike spoke, the man nodded to his companions to spread out.

They strode across the room toward Reaper and Wrath.

Reaper stood his ground with Wrath right beside him. "Think you can deal with the two on our right?" Reaper asked tensely.

"I'll give it a shot," Wrath replied.

A guy in his late teens swung the bat he was carrying. Wrath danced back, ducked then lunged forward, slashing his knife across the teen's leg.

"They got knives," the teen cried out.

"Not for long," one of them said, bringing the pipe he was holding down on Wrath's arm.

Reaper was doing his best to avoid the weapons the three other men held. He sidestepped one, grabbed it and managed to yank it from the young man's hand. Instantly, he used it against his foe, landing a hard blow to his side that had the guy shouting in pain while backing away to avoid another hit.

Mike, who appeared to be the leader, swung the golf club he was holding. Before Reaper could move or defend himself, it struck his shoulder. His arm went numb momentarily, but he managed to switch his knife to his other hand. Spinning quickly to avoid being hit by the third of his assailants, he kicked out, hard. The attacker screamed in pain when Reaper's boot connected with his groin.

"One down for the count," Reaper muttered to himself.

The man fell to the floor, curling in a fetal position to protect his damaged balls.

"Want to try that with me?" Mike said menacingly, lifting the club again.

Reaper dodged away only to find himself facing another teen, who was holding a bat.

"Homerun," the teen cried out gleefully when the bat cracked hard against Reaper's thigh.

"Out!" Reaper ignored the pain as he managed to stab the knife into the teen's side and twist the blade before pulling it out.

The teen looked at him in shock, dropping the bat to cover his bloody wound with one hand. Then he turned and ran. That left only the leader for Reaper to deal with.

Wrath was having problems of his own. His left arm hung useless by his side, his knife lay on the ground, and his two attackers were closing in for the kill.

"Need some help?" Zip sped across the room, closely followed by Colly and Raven.

They all carried short lengths of pipe. Zip used his to whack Johnny hard across his head. He fell back, right into Wrath. Wrath took advantage of that to bring his knee up between Johnny's legs and the attacker went down.

Colly snagged Wrath's knife from the rubbish on the floor. "Want a piece of me?" he said in a passable imitation of Al Pacino, lunging at the second of Wrath's attackers. The teen, already bleeding from the wound in his leg Wrath had inflicted, turned tail, heading for the door to make his escape.

Mike had managed to hit Reaper again with the golf club by that time—a glancing blow to Reaper's hip that had Reaper falling to his knees.

Reaper held his knife, looking for an opening, when suddenly Raven jumped on the assailant's back. "Get him, Reaper," she shouted, obviously holding on for dear life as Mike tried to shake her off.

Afraid he might stab her instead, Reaper dropped the knife and hurtled forward from his kneeling position. His head caught Mike in his chest, sending him and Raven to the floor in a pile of arms and legs, with Reaper on top of them.

"Goddamn it, get off of me!" Raven shouted, trying to wriggle out from under the pile.

Reaper helped her by grabbing Mike's upper arms and rolling sideways. She slithered free, crawled to get the knife, and stabbed it into Mike's bicep.

"Whoops," she muttered when it also cut Reaper's hand.

"I'll live," Reaper told her. He spotted the golf club and snagged it while Mike tried to stem the flow of blood from his wound. Holding the club in both hands, Reaper managed to straddle him and press the shaft of the club against his throat. "You even think of moving," Reaper growled, "and I'll break your neck."

"Do it," Zip called out. "We'll help, once we get this bastard tied up." He held up a short length of rope, pointing to the man he'd cold-cocked. Colly rolled the guy onto his stomach so Zip could tie his arms behind his back.

"Naw. I can think of something better to do with him," Raven said gleefully. "Move up a bit, Reaper."

When he did, so that he was sitting on Mike's chest, she undid the assailant's belt then pulled his jeans down around his ankles. Zip was beside her seconds later. Between them, they got Mike's shoes and jeans off him.

Reaper debated momentarily then moved the club and landed a hard blow to Mike's jaw. "That should hold him," he said, as he tried to stand. Pain shot through his leg, crumpling him to the floor.

"How bad?" Wrath asked, hobbling over to Reaper. He was holding his injured arm curled tightly against his chest as he knelt beside Reaper.

"I could ask the same," Reaper replied.

"Not broken, I don't think. Probably fractured."

"We have to get them to the ER," Raven said.

"Not happening," Wrath told her.

"But," she protested.

"We'll go to the free clinic, where they won't question us," Reaper said, trying again to get to his feet. Colly wrapped his arm around Reaper, steadying him. "First, though, we have to deal with the trash." Reaper pointed to their foes.

"I didn't see a Dumpster when we came in." Wrath managed a smile, despite his obvious pain. "So I'll call this in."

"Nope," Reaper replied with a hard shake of his head.

"Not as me, you dope. I'm not quite that out of it. But let's get out of here first, just in case my boys in blue show up in record time."

With the teens' help, they made it from the building down to the sidewalk at the end of the alley. Then Wrath called in a 10-78 — need assistance — and gave the address. He ended the call quickly, handing it to Zip. "Break it and toss it. It's my throwaway. Dispatch will think the call was from one of our undercover guys."

Zip seemed to get a kick out of smashing it under his shoe before picking up the pieces then dropping them through a storm grate.

"How did you guys happen to show up there?" Reaper asked as they walked slowly to where he'd parked the car.

"Maxie said you were looking for us and that he'd sent you to the warehouse, since we said that's where we were going. We would have been there before you, but we ran into a couple of dudes we knew and..." He shrugged.

Colly grinned. "At least we got there before the end and got our licks in. Hell, if we hadn't—"

"We might have been dead meat, literally," Reaper said with a sour smile. "Guess I'm getting too old for this."

"Not even," Raven retorted. "You're Reaper. You'll be doing this forever."

Reaper snorted. "I'm not some superhero, girl. Neither of us is."

"But you *can't* quit. Who'll take over for you?" Zip said.

Reaper didn't reply for a moment. He bit back pain when he stepped wrong as he turned the corner into the almost deserted lot where he'd left his old beater. His leg started to buckle, and Colly caught him, helping him the rest of the way to the car. With the teens' assistance, Reaper and Wrath got into the front seat. Then, at Reaper's insistence, Raven and the guys got in back.

"You sure you can drive?" Zip asked. "I'm too young to die in a car accident."

"I'll manage." Reaper started the car then slowly pulled out of the lot and onto the street. Every movement of his leg caused pain, even more so now that the adrenalin was wearing off, but he was damned if he was going to let anyone know it.

"Why do you want us with you?" Raven said, leaning over the back of the seat. "And you better hurry. I think Wrath's worse off than he looks."

Reaper took a worried glance, noting how pale Wrath was, and stepped on the accelerator. "I wanted you here," Reaper said in reply to Raven's question, "because of what Zip said."

"That I don't want to be in a crash? I think that was a given."

"No." Reaper managed a grin. "About who'll take over when Wrath and I retire." He took a right, heading to the free clinic. "You three did a damn good job tonight."

"Yeah. So? We're used to defending ourselves against crapazoids like those guys. Well, maybe not Raven so much." He pulled back when she took a disgusted swipe at him.

She grumbled, "I held my own. Mostly."

"Yes, you did," Reaper agreed. "So what I was thinking — and this is off the cuff — with some training, you three could do what we're doing."

"You're shitting us," Colly said.

"Nope. You know what to look out for, and you wouldn't stand out until it was too late for the punks trying to cause trouble to know you're around."

"Yeah, but…" Raven looked skeptical.

"It's just an idea. Think about it." By then they were in front of the clinic. Reaper could see lights on, even at this late hour. After parking, everyone got out. Colly helped Reaper up the steps while Zip and Raven walked beside Wrath. After ringing the doorbell, they waited for someone to answer. The door opened a minute later, revealing a dark-skinned man dressed in whites. He took one look at Reaper and Wrath and called for assistance. A nurse appeared and between them and the teens, they got Reaper and Wrath into exam rooms.

* * * *

"Did the kids leave?" Zack asked when Dallas came into exam room.

"Yeah. I told them there was no sense in their hanging around. Oh, by the way, we're both undercover cops, as far as the docs here know. They think the guys brought us here because they thought we were homeless." Then he whistled softly. "That doesn't look good."

"At least I'm not in a cast," Zack retorted, seeing one on Dallas' arm, since the doctor had cut the sleeves off his sweatshirt to get to it. "I thought you said it wasn't broken."

"It's not. But I still need the cast for a few weeks according to the doctor, until the fracture heals." Looking at the huge bruise on Zack's thigh, he asked, "Are you able to walk?"

"Not without crutches for a day or two," the doctor said, coming into the room. "This," he told Zack, "is a compression bandage. You'll be using this except when you're icing the bruise." As he talked, he began wrapping the bandage around Zack's thigh, starting at his knee and working up. "Keep it snug, but not too tight. It keeps the swelling out of the muscle tissue."

"For how long?"

"The bandage and icing? Until the pain diminishes and the muscle begins to heal. That usually takes about forty-eight hours. Then you can start exercising the muscles, but carefully. No pushing through the pain.

Luckily for you, your coat and sweatshirts kept your shoulder from sustaining more than minor bruising." When he finished with the bandage, he stepped back, looking Zack. "Do you mind my asking what happened?"

Going with what Dallas had told the doctors, Zack replied, "We were looking for a pair of men who prey on the homeless. Unfortunately for us, it seems they recruited a few others to join their fun and games."

The doctor looked at him dubiously. "You weren't armed?"

"We were," Dallas said, "but we didn't get a chance to draw on them when they jumped us, since our guns were in our boots. And before you ask, we left them locked in the car rather than bringing them in here with us."

"How did those kids get involved?"

"Wrong place, wrong time, but if they hadn't walked in on the fight, we might not have made it out alive," Zack told him.

"Sort of makes what you went through worth it, doesn't it? Knowing there are street kids out there willing to step in when necessary. I hope you managed to arrest the punks."

"It's been taken care of," Dallas said.

"Can we leave now?" Zack asked.

"As soon as I write you prescriptions for pain killers and antibiotics and get you some crutches."

"I know this is a free clinic," Zack said, "but given the circumstances, we'll pay if you give us a bill."

"Thank you. Believe me, that will be greatly appreciated."

Twenty minutes later, Dallas and Zack were back at the car after Zack had gotten a short lesson on using crutches then paid the bill.

"Can you drive with one arm?" Zack asked, handing Dallas the keys.

"I'll manage. You get in back so you can keep your leg up, the way the doc ordered."

"That was the plan," Zack said dryly.

It took some maneuvering, but Zack managed to get into the back seat, thankful that the shot the doctor had given him for the pain had kicked in. He realized he must have dozed off when he felt Dallas gently shake his shoulder some time later.

"We're home."

Once Zack was out of the car, he said, as he made his way to the back door of the house, "I'm glad we're here before Mrs. Cook."

Dallas laughed. "Because she'll start mothering you?"

"And you, so don't be so cocky. But more because of the way we're dressed. This is *not* how she's used to seeing us."

"True that," Dallas agreed.

They were still in the clothes they'd been wearing before the fight. Clothes that were now even more ripped and torn—and bloody.

By the time they reached the bedroom, Zack had gained a greater appreciation for how well Brian managed on crutches, and said as much to Dallas.

"Well, he has been on them forever," Dallas pointed out, while struggling to get undressed with one hand.

It took Zack's able, if careful assistance, to remove the sweatshirt and T-shirt he was wearing. After that, things were easier and soon they were in bed.

"Don't you have to call in to tell them you're not coming to work?" Zack asked drowsily.

"It's Thursday. I'm off, thank goodness. But you'd better let Alice know you're not going to be there."

"Damn." Zack took the phone from the charger and called his office, leaving her a long message, asking her to reschedule his appointments because he'd been in a minor car accident.

"That works," Dallas said when Zack hung up. "I'll use that excuse too when I go in tomorrow. At least I have a few days leave coming so I can take them and not end up on desk duty." He shuddered, earning him a sleepy chuckle from Zack.

Very carefully, they curled up together, kissed and soon fell asleep. But not before saying, in unison, "I love you."

Chapter Twenty

"What the hell happened to you?" Brian asked, when he opened the door to let Zack and Dallas in to his house Saturday evening. "Or shouldn't I ask?"

"Let's just say we ran into a bit of trouble the night before last."

"From the looks of it, it was more than a bit," Brian commented as he wheeled into the living room. "Have a seat before you fall on your face."

Zack snorted. "I'm getting the hang of these, finally," he told Brian, setting the crutches beside the sofa and sitting.

Dallas settled at the other end, where he could rest his cast on the arm of the sofa.

"So what's this big news?" Zack asked, although he was certain he knew the answer.

"We're ready to start painting then get everything moved from the old building to the new one. I was going to have you round up a few of the kids you know to help, but under the circumstances…"

"That's great. When do you need them?" Zack took out the phone he used for Zip and the others.

"Tomorrow?"

"You got it." He punched in Zip's number, and when the teen answered, Zack told him what was needed. He smiled at something Zip said and told him he'd ask. Covering the phone, he said to Brian, "You'll probably have more kids than you need. Especially if they can do it at night, so they'll be warm for eight hours. The way the weather is right now, that's a definite enticement, if you're willing."

"Hell, yes, I am."

Zack relayed Brian's reply then hung up after telling Zip he'd be back in touch with details.

"Of course," Brian said, scrubbing his forehead, "I'll have to find a couple of counselors willing to supervise at night."

"Nope. Dallas and I can do that. It's not like we're in any shape yet to get back out there doing our vigilante thing."

"And won't be for a while," Dallas added, shooting Zack a hard look.

Brian chuckled. "Knowing Zack, he wants to be out there before the week is up."

"No shit, but it's not happening. And that is doctor's orders, not mine."

"I know," Zack said gloomily. "At least we can be useful at the building in the interim."

"You'll survive," Brian replied, reaching over to pat his knee.

"Yeah, I know." Suddenly Zack had an idea. One he would put forward to Dallas after they left. He knew if he said anything in front of Brian, he'd get a lecture and a half about it, and why he was even planning such a thing to begin with.

After Brian offered them beers — that they accepted — Zack asked, "Exactly what needs doing on the building, Brian, that the kids will be able to handle?"

The three men spent some time making detailed plans on how to proceed with the painting and other minor things within the scope of the kids' abilities. Then they chatted for a few minutes more before Brian told Zack and Dallas in no uncertain terms that they should go home and get some sleep.

"You'll need it," he said with a laugh. "Supervising a dozen kids is not the easiest thing you've ever done. Trust me on this one."

* * * *

"I don't see why not," Dallas said as they drove home from Brian's place. "The problem is that we're in no shape to do it."

"What they need is training on the finer points of attack and defense. They know the basics just from trying to stay safe out there." Zack tapped his lip pensively. "I know a man who might be willing to teach them, if he's still around. It's been a few years since I last saw him."

Dallas cocked an eyebrow. "An ex-client?"

"Nope. A guy who showed me a thing or two, back when I was on the streets."

"Damn, Zack, that was over twenty years ago. He could be dead and gone by now."

"I'm still here and he was only a few years older than me." Zack took out his phone as they talked. "He used to hang around at Spars."

"And you think someone will remember him now?"

"Worth a shot." Zack punched in the number for the gym. When the call was answered, he asked if the owner was around.

After a moment on hold, a man said, "Jim here. Can I help you?"

"I'm looking for an old friend I've lost track of, Nate Brown. I know he used to work out there sometimes."

After a pause, Jim replied, "Name rings a bell. If he's who I'm thinking of, he started his own gym, Rattlers he calls it, because that was his street name. It's up north of the city."

"That's him. Thanks."

"No problem. If you find him, tell him I said hello."

"Will do." Zack hung up then looked up Rattlers. "Feel like taking the long way home?"

"How long?" When Zack gave him the address, Dallas nodded. "I know right where it is. Mike took me up there once to work off some steam after a really bad night. The guy who owns it was there. Talk about one bad motherfucker. I bet he could take on Arreola and win."

"Sure, if you say so."

Dallas laughed. "You have no clue, do you?"

"I'd guess he's a boxer, and you know I'm not a boxing fan. I didn't know you were, though."

"Not really, but some of the guys are, so I pick up on things."

They bantered a bit about various sports neither of them really cared about until they arrived at the gym. Zack picked up on a few pitying glances when they went inside. It didn't surprise him since he and Dallas still looked like the walking wounded with him on crutches and Dallas wearing a cast.

When he got to a counter at one side of the gym, Zack asked the guy manning it, "Is Nate around?"

"Maybe. Who wants to know?"

"Tell him Zack's looking for him."

"You found him," a booming voice said from behind Zack and Dallas.

Zack turned and was engulfed in a bear hug that made him drop his crutches. Then the man released him, looking him over from head to toe.

"Who the hell did you run into? I thought I taught you better than to end up looking like you went a few rounds with a kangaroo." Nate picked up the crutches then handed them to Zack. "Who's your friend?" He turned to Dallas. "You in the same fight?"

"I was. I'm Dallas."

"Dallas, Dallas. Yeah, I sorta remember you. You were here with Mike once. You're not bad"—Nate tapped Dallas' cast—"but not perfect either. "So, Zack, what happened and why are you here?"

"We need your help, if you're willing. And not against the punks we ran into. They're already taken care of."

"Hope they look worse than you two. Come on. Let's go into my office."

Zack and Dallas followed him into a large room that obviously served as both an office and a place to store extra equipment. Once they were all seated around the desk on one side of the room, Zack told Nate a bit about what had gone on in his life since they'd been together twenty years ago.

"So," Nate said, grinning. "You're the infamous Reaper. I'm proud of you, kid." He ran a hand over his short, graying hair. "So how can I help?"

"I have some kids... Not mine," Zack added when he realized how that could be taken. "Homeless teens who I think could step in and take over for me, if they get some training. They're pretty good at defending themselves, but that's different from going after the kind of punks who prey on street kids."

Nate tapped his fingers together. "How many and how old?"

"Right now, three. Two guys and a girl. All in their late teens."

"A girl?"

"Come on, Nate," Dallas said, "don't be chauvinistic. Girls can fight just as well as guys."

"Hell, I know that. My old lady can handle half the men who work out here. I take it these kids know you as Reaper," Nate said.

"Reaper and Wrath," Zack replied with a nod to Dallas. "A few others know too, and they're keeping it on the QT."

"Okay. So, when do you want to do this?"

"That depends. I could bring them here, of course."

"But? It sounds like there is one."

"The three of them are going to be helping out, along with some of their friends, painting and such, at the new home for Off-the-Street."

"Yeah, I heard they have to move the shelter. So you were hoping I could come down there to teach them?"

"If you're willing. I know it's asking a lot."

"Hell, kid. For you, I'll do it."

Dallas chortled. "He's hardly a kid anymore."

"Yeah, well to me that's what he'll always be. The kid I taught to defend himself better than he had been. Not that he was a slouch at it, but..." He patted Zack's shoulder. "Now the kid is all grown up and dealing out some hurt to those who deserve it. I like that idea. When do you want me down there?"

"Tomorrow evening?"

"You got it. Just tell me where."

Zack gave him the address before asking Nate, "So what's new with you these days?"

Nate told him the latest, especially about his wife and family.

Finally, realizing it was getting late, Zack suggested it was time to get home. He and Dallas left with Nate's promise that he'd see them the next night at the building.

* * * *

"Holy shit, that dude is scary," Zip said when he came up from the basement of the new Off-the-Street.

He, Colly, Raven and a fourth teen Zip had recruited, who called himself Sway, were working with Nate on their fighting skills.

"I know," Reaper replied. "I told you he's the one who taught me, way back when. You look like you're surviving, though."

"Yeah. Am. He sent me up for" — Zip hurried over to the large cooler by counter to grab five bottles of water — "these." Seconds later, he vanished down the stairs again.

Chuckling, Reaper went back to what he was doing — supervising a team of teens who were painting the walls on the first floor. "And the floors and themselves," he grumbled before reminding them that there was only so much paint available, so they should be a bit less enthusiastic when wielding the rollers and brushes.

It was close to midnight when he called a halt for the night. Wrath came downstairs, followed by half a dozen teens, to announce that all the rooms on the third floor were finished. Admittedly, a quarter of them, plus those on the second floor, had already been painted when he and Reaper had arrived around six to take over from the counselors and kids who had been working during the day.

"Who's up for pizza before crashing for the night?" Reaper asked the gathered throng.

"Who isn't would probably be the right question," Nate said, as he and his trainees joined the group.

Reaper counted heads then called a pizza delivery chain to order enough pizzas that the guy who answered the phone asked if this was some kind of prank. Reaper assured him it wasn't, and gave him his credit card number to prove it. Aside from the pizzas, Reaper ordered drinks and asked for napkins and paper plates as well.

While they waited, Wrath suggested the kids clean up. Some of them grabbed their backpacks from where they'd left them, heading up to the bathrooms. Others went to use the kitchen sinks.

"So how did it go?" Reaper asked Nate, now that they were alone for a moment.

"You've got a good team. Raven..." Nate grinned. "You wouldn't think it to look at her but she held her own when I had them working in pairs against each other."

"Figured she would. What about Sway? He's one I never ran into."

"He's got the brawn. He just has to learn a bit more self-control. I told them we should get together a couple more times to practice what I showed them. Okay if we do that here tomorrow night?"

"As far as I know, it is. I'll call Brian in the morning, just to be certain. Since the painting is all but finished, I think carpeting is next on the list then he'll start moving everything over from the old building."

A loud banging on the front door, plus a few of the teens coming back into the room, put an end to their conversation. Nate let the pizza deliveryman in, then he sent Zip and Colly out to help him bring in the order. They spread the boxes out on the new admitting counter and soon all the kids were sitting on the floor to eat while Reaper, Wrath and Nate used the counter as their table.

When everyone was finished and the garbage collected into a large trash bag, Reaper said, "We're leaving now. I know all of you will behave. Right?" He got loud assents from all the teens. "Do not open the door to anyone, and that includes friends. Got that?" Again, he got cries of agreement.

"Okay, everyone. Upstairs," Wrath said.

At his order, the kids grabbed their backpacks and headed to the second floor. When they were out of earshot, he asked, "You sure it's safe to leave them here on their own?"

Nate and Reaper both nodded. Nate said, "They know this place is important for them and for every other kid out on the streets. None of them will do anything stupid. Besides…" He grinned. "My team will make damn good and sure no one misbehaves."

"Your team?" Reaper chuckled.

"Yeah. They tagged themselves The R&W Rattlers."

Wrath snorted. "I thought R&W was a root beer."

"It's A&W, nut," Reaper told him.

"Ah, right. Guess I'm tired."

"Then let's go home." Reaper went to the bottom of the stairs then shouted up, "We're leaving."

He got a chorus of "Good night" in return.

After turning out the lights on the ground floor, Zack adjusted his crutches—for the hundredth time, it seemed to him—and the three men headed out.

Chapter Twenty-One

"Is it a bit too much?" Brian asked Thursday morning, gazing up at the banner above the door of the new Off-the-Street.

All the work had been finished, and everything from the old building had been moved over the previous day.

"Well," Zack chuckled. "It does sort of remind me of the first day of a new supermarket."

The banner said 'Grand Opening' in blazing red and gold graffiti-style lettering, and was obviously handmade.

"Yeah I know, but the kids insisted that we needed it and when I protested, ten of them got together to make that."

"It's definitely eye-catching," Dallas commented. "Enough to draw crowds."

Zack nodded, looking at the line of homeless kids waiting for Brian to unlock the door to the new home for the shelter. Before Brian could, a limousine pulled up in front of the building. The chauffeur got out then opened the rear door, and the mayor, flanked by two subordinates, stepped onto the sidewalk. Moments later, two more cars arrived, disgorging members of the city council. Photographers and TV cameramen converged and began shooting the scene as the dignitaries came over to congratulate a somewhat nonplused Brian.

Zack and Dallas rapidly moved away to join Nate and the Rattlers, who were standing next to the building.

"I didn't expect this to be a circus," Dallas muttered.

"From the look on Brian's face, neither did he. I can't say that I'm too surprised, however," Zack replied. "The paper had a big article on the City page this morning about the shelter's new home and that it would be opening today."

By then, more city dignitaries had appeared. Most of the teens had faded away at that point. Zack was certain it was because they didn't want to be photographed for fear their families might see them in the paper or on television.

"You're sticking around?" Zack asked Zip and the others.

Raven shrugged, replying, "My folks are halfway across the country. I don't think this will make the national news."

"Same here," Colly told Zack.

"And me and Sway are legal age," Zip put in, "so there's nothing our families can do, even if they gave a damn."

Zack watched, torn between amusement and pity as Brian dealt with mayor and reporters. Then, with a flourish, Brian turned, unlocked the door, and ushered everyone inside. Twenty minutes or so later, the dignitaries dispersed, their photo-op time over. The TV and newspersons followed, and things were quiet for the moment. Zack and the others went inside to find

Brian leaning against the counter, talking to three of the counselors.

"We've survived Armageddon," Brian said with a small grin when he saw Zack.

"Now comes part two," Zack replied, as some of the homeless kids, who had been outside before the invasion, began to reappear. Soon Brian and his staff were busy dealing with them.

"Time for us to get out of here," Zack said to Dallas. "I have to get to work, and you —"

"Get to go home and enjoy the rest of my day off."

"What about us?" Zip asked.

"Go help out," Nate told him. "I think they could use a hand."

"Hang on." Zack beckoned for the Rattlers to follow him back outside. "Tonight, you're coming with us," he told them when they were assembled on the sidewalk a few yards from the shelter's front door.

The teens looked both excited and scared. "Where do we meet?" Raven asked.

"Before you tell her, Zack, are you and him" — Nate nodded toward Dallas — "in shape yet?"

"I'll use the cast to cold-cock any punks we run into," Dallas said with a grin, earning him a disgusted look from Zack.

"I'm doing okay," Zack told Nate. "As you can see, I'm not on the crutches. I am taking it easy, but I can walk, obviously. I'll just be an observer if anything goes down."

Nate nodded. "I'll come along too — to observe."

"Thanks," Zack replied. "How about we all meet at one a.m. behind the old shelter building?"

"Cool," Sway said. "Now can we go back inside? There's food, and I'm starving."

Laughing, Zack told them all to move it before there was nothing left to eat.

"See you tonight," Nate said as they walked to where they'd parked their cars.

Since Dallas had done the driving, he dropped Zack off at the office, telling him he'd be back at five to pick him up, then he went home.

* * * *

"Remember," Reaper said, "the idea is to stop the predators before they do any real damage to whoever they're attacking." He looked at each of the Rattlers one by one, getting nods in return. "Use their own weapons against them whenever possible. The element of surprise is crucial. Usually they will be so intent on hurting their victim, they won't realize you're there until it's too late, if you move in silently."

"I have this," Sway said, taking a small knife from his jacket pocket.

Colly also had one that he showed Reaper.

"Only use them if things become serious, like they did at the warehouse. The basic idea is to either scare the punks into giving up and leaving, or disarming them. Without" — again he looked from Rattler to Rattler — "getting hurt yourselves."

"You knew the basics," Nate put in. "I taught you a few more tricks. Use them and you'll come out on top."

"One last thing," Wrath said. "No matter how pissed off you are — and you will be — you have to remember you're there to save the victim. Do *not* to take out your hatred of all the bastards who prey on kids like you by beating the ones you run into to a pulp if you get the chance. Strip them of the bats or whatever they're using, chase them off then help the victim."

"Okay, enough lecturing," Reaper said. "You have two choices. All four of you go out together, or you break into two teams. My suggestion is two and two. You can cover more area that way, and you'll be less conspicuous." When the teens decided on teams, Reaper said, "Good. I'll go with you two." He pointed to Zip and Colly. "Wrath will stick with Raven and Sway. Nate?" He looked at him.

Nate glanced at Wrath's cast and replied, "That's a no-brainer. I'm with him and his."

Wrath grinned. "Hey, I told you my cast is a weapon of mass destruction."

"Get that out of your head right now," Reaper muttered. "Besides which, we're only observing. This is the Rattlers game now."

"Not a game," Zip said seriously. "This is for real."

"Yeah, it is. Never forget that," Reaper agreed. "Okay, let's do it. We'll meet back here at dawn."

* * * *

"Slow night, not that there's a damned thing wrong with that," Reaper said, when he and the others reconvened just as the sun was coming up.

"We did stop two guys roughing up a kid who was dealing," Sway said. "Seems like they didn't want to pay for their weed. We taught them—as my bitch of a mom used to put it—the error of their ways."

"We didn't stop someone from getting hurt... Well, maybe we did. There was a girl, about sixteen, with a younger one, maybe ten. I think the older one was keeping the kid safe, you know." Zip told the others. "So anyway, this son of a bitch older dude in a car pulls over, gets out and starts following them, and they know he's there and duck into an alley, which wasn't too smart 'cause he starts to go after them. We got in his face, had a little talk with him, chased him off," Zip said proudly.

"Then we found them, told them about the shelter. Not sure they'll go there, but..." Colly added with a shrug. "We did try."

"That's the best you could have done," Nate said, patting his back.

Reaper nodded. "And with luck, the guy will think twice before trolling the neighborhood again."

"You know what?" Raven said. "We should get berets like those guys in...somewhere or another, have."

Wrath shook his head. "You're trying *not* to stand out."

"Yeah? Well, look at how Reaper did it before you joined him. All leather and tough looking."

"But that was just me out on my own," Reaper pointed out. "You guys do something to show you're out there being protectors and you'll become targets for every punk who's looking for trouble."

"So? Then we deal with them. That's the idea. Right?"

"Do you think you can handle four or five ganging up on you, because they don't like that you're around, ruining their fun?"

Raven sighed. "Probably not. Okay, we'll keep it on the down low."

Reaper smiled. "Good. Now who's hungry? I'm buying." He wasn't in the least surprised when all the Rattlers cheered, so they went to Frank's Place, ate, then they split up.

The teens headed to Off-the-Street, hoping to be able to crash there for the day.

Nate gave them a high-five before they left, saying, "You guys did even better than I hoped. I'm proud of you. And now, I'm off to catch a couple of hours sleep."

"Wish we could do that," Reaper said with a rueful smile before he and Dallas headed back to the house to change clothes and go to their day jobs.

Chapter Twenty-Two

"Home sweet home," Dallas said, a month after the Rattlers first foray into protecting the homeless of Uptown. He settled next to Zack on the sofa with a sigh of relief.

Zack grinned, giving him a kiss. "Tired?" When Dallas nodded, Zack told him, "Then rest and unwind. We have nothing that needs doing until morning."

"Do you miss the excitement?" Dallas asked.

"It's only been two weeks since we stopped keeping an eye on the kids and hung it up for good. Right now, I'm enjoying being able to spend a lot more time with you."

Dallas arched one eyebrow. "Only right now? Do you expect that to change in the near future?"

"What do you think?" Zack asked, pulling him against his chest.

Dallas turned his head to look at him. "I think that was a stupid question."

"It was," Zack agreed before kissing him soundly. "As for your original question. Yeah, I do a little, but not enough to go back to it again. The kids are doing a good job. They don't need us hanging around. Besides, I'm too old to be out playing vigilante."

"You're only as old as you feel up here," Dallas said, tapping Zack's forehead.

"Tell that to my body," Zack grumbled.

"Trust me. There's nothing wrong with your body. I should know. I see it every day. It's almost perfect."

"For an older—"

Dallas stopped him with a kiss before saying, "Will you quit with that? You're forty-one, not ninety." Resting his head on Zack's shoulder, he looked off into space for a long moment. "You know what you need? What we *both* need?"

"Do I want to know?"

"Maybe. I was thinking, how about we take a vacation? We've never done that. Between our jobs and your nighttime activities, it just didn't happen. Now it can, if you're willing."

"You can get the time off?"

"Yep. I've got two weeks of vacation time this year, and that doesn't count what I've accrued over the last few years that I haven't used."

Zack chuckled. "So you could get a whole month or three?"

"Technically, but I don't think the lieutenant would go for that."

"Probably not. Okay, you find out when, and we'll go from there. I can take my laptop with us in case any of my clients need to consult me."

"No. Way. In. Hell! This is going to be a *real* vacation. Not a working one. If your clients can't fend for themselves for a week…"

"I know," Zack said, giving him a hug. "I was teasing—mostly."

"Good. But just to be certain, I'm going to find us somewhere to go that doesn't have wireless service."

"Not possible."

"Bet me." Dallas got up and went into their home office to boot up the computer. He typed in 'vacation spots with no cell phone service' in the search engine.

Zack watched, shaking his head. "Bet you don't find anything."

"What are you willing to bet?"

"I'll take you out to dinner tonight to 'our favorite Italian restaurant if I'm wrong."

"You're on." Hitting the search icon, Dallas grinned when the first page of dozens popped up. He clicked on the top item and when it opened, he scrolled through the suggestions. "How do you feel about boats? Not cruises but sailing?"

"Never tried it."

"So that's one idea." Dallas continued scrolling. "Or this one." He tapped the screen.

Zack read what it said and nodded. "Now that I like—a lot."

"Then let's do it." Dallas grinned. "You owe me dinner. And"—his grinned widened—"this place has an added advantage. It's only half a day from my parent's house."

"You set me up," Zack muttered, but he was smiling.

"Only a little."

Dallas got his dinner.

Three weeks later, the pair would take off on their first-ever vacation together.

* * * *

"So this is the infamous Zack." The man standing on the front porch of the small, white-shingled house had his arms crossed over his chest as he studied Zack.

"I am, sir," Zack replied, shooting a worried look at Dallas.

"George," the petite, gray-haired woman standing beside him admonished. "Behave, and be friendly." She hurried down the stairs to hug Dallas. "It's about time you brought him home to meet us."

George Comstock grinned, coming down to join his wife. "I figured I should at least make an attempt to play the worried father, meeting his son's—I believe the term these days is significant other. It's good to finally meet you, Zack."

He held out his hand, and Zack shook it.

"The pretty lady, as I'm certain you've surmised, is Pattie, my wife."

"It's a pleasure to meet you too, sir."

"It's George, and don't you forget it," George grumbled. "We don't stand on formalities around here."

"And you had best call me Pattie," Mrs. Comstock told Zack. "Or Mom, like Dallas does." She smiled at her son. "You are being way too quiet. Cat got your tongue?"

"Nope. Just wanted to let the three of you do the intro thing without my interfering. So"—he hugged his mother—"I don't suppose you have any coffee made. I'm dying here."

"Only because you wouldn't stop when I suggested we get some," Zack told him.

"I wanted us to get here before you backed out and commandeered the car to take us straight to the lake."

"I wouldn't."

Dallas grinned as they followed his parents into the house. "You were thinking about it."

"Was not."

"Boys, quit arguing," Pattie said. "I have coffee, and some of the strudel you like so much, Dallas." She led the way into the kitchen then urged them to sit.

"Now that you're finally here, Zack," George said while they waited for Pattie to make coffee and set out plates for the strudel, "tell us all about yourself. All Dallas has said it that you're an investment counselor, and that you two started living together soon after you met. Well..." George smiled. "He went into a bit more detail than that, but not by much."

"For instance, he never told us much about your family. Where do they live and have they met Dallas?" Pattie asked.

Zack looked at Dallas for help.

"I didn't tell you about them," Dallas said, "because they're not part of his life and haven't been for a long time."

"They're dead. Oh, dear. I'm so sorry, Zack," Pattie said, giving him a quick hug.

"No, they're still alive as far as I know," Zack replied. After taking a deep breath, he explained why.

When Zack finished, there was a long silence.

Then George replied, "From the sound of it, you're much better off without them. You've made something of yourself and should be proud that you did. We can't, not to be trite, choose our family. We can choose to do the best possible with the life we've been given, and from what Dallas has told us about you, you've done exactly that."

"Thank you," Zack said. "I owe a lot of it to Dallas." He took Dallas' hand, squeezing it.

Dallas snorted. "You were already rich and famous when I met you."

"Rich?" George looked at Zack, a twinkle in his eye. "So you're able to keep our son in the life he was never accustomed to?"

Everyone broke into laughter at that. Then Pattie poured the coffee, put out the strudel, and they spent the rest of the morning with Dallas and his parents catching up on what had happened since the last time they'd talked. They also showed Zack around the house.

"This is the jewelry box I told you about," Dallas said at one point. "The one I made Mom in woodshop."

Since it was a simple hinged box with carved leaves on the top and sides, Zack knew it must mean a lot to her to have it sitting on her dressing table all these years later.

"I've treasured it like it was made of pure gold," Pattie told Zack proudly.

"Well you should." For a moment, Zack felt a tug of self-pity that his life hadn't been such that he could have made something like it for his mother — and have her display it as proudly as Pattie did the jewelry box. Then he pushed that to the back of his mind where it belonged.

Dallas must have read something in Zack's expression. Wrapping his arm around Zack's waist, he said quietly, "Now you have a *new* family."

"Indeed, he does," Pattie said emphatically, smiling in delight. "And we have a second son."

Dallas looked at Zack, and they both broke out laughing. "How about you don't call him that, Mom," Dallas said. "It conjures up images I'm not sure I can deal with."

It took Pattie a second to get what he meant, then she laughed too. "All right. The... No, that doesn't work either."

"The boy next door who spent all his time hanging around here, so we thought of him as a second son," George suggested.

"That works," Dallas said.

They all agreed it did.

After that, they went out into the backyard where George barbecued burgers and hotdogs for lunch. There was potato salad and ice cream as well, and by the time the meal was over, everyone was happily sated.

Then, since it was getting late, and Zack and Dallas still had to drive to the lake, where the boat they were renting waited, they said their goodbyes.

"Promise you'll come back soon," Pattie said, giving Zack a tight hug. "Maybe for Christmas?"

"We will, if Dallas can get the time off."

"You had better," George said, giving Dallas a stern look.

"I will, I will." Dallas hugged his father then his mom. "Love you both."

"We love you too. And I'm pretty sure... No, I *know* we love Zack as well," Pattie replied, kissing Zack's cheek.

As they drove away from the house, Zack sighed contentedly. "They are good people. But then I figured that they would be. They raised one of the best men I've ever met."

"One of?" Dallas said with a mock pout.

"Okay. *The* best man. The one I love, heart and soul."

"Back at you," Dallas replied, reaching over to hold Zack's hand. "Now, and forever."

* * * *

"And we actually relaxed and unwound," Zack commented when their vacation was over and they'd returned to the city. "Now, back to the grind." He smiled, adding, "Until Christmas."

Sometimes, but not often, they missed being Reaper and Wrath. But as Dallas pointed out, "We made the right choice. The Rattlers replaced us quite admirably."

And, Zack added, smiling, "The new Off-the-Street is serving more of the homeless community in Uptown than even Brian had thought possible."

"Life is good," Zack said softly late one evening as he and Dallas cuddled in bed. "We made a difference and now —"

"We can be just us," Dallas replied. "Two men with the time, finally, to show just how much we love each other."

"And there's not a damn thing wrong with that."

About the Author

Born and bred Cleveland, I earned a degree in technical theater, later switched to costuming and headed to NYC. Finally seeing the futility of trying to become rich and famous in the Big Apple, I joined VISTA (Volunteers in Service to America), ending up in Chicago for three years. Then it was on to Denver where I put down roots and worked as a costume designer until just recently.

I began writing a few years ago after joining an online fanfic group. Two friends and I then started a group for writers where they may post any story they wish no matter the genre or content. Since then, for the last three years, I've been writing for publication. Most, but not all, of my work is m/m, either mildly erotic or purely 'romantic', and more often than not it involves a mystery or covert operations.

Edward Kendrick loves to hear from readers. You can find his contact information, website and author biography at http://www.pride-publishing.com

www.ingramcontent.com/pod-product-compliance
Lightning Source LLC
Chambersburg PA
CBHW020423180626
46812CB00003B/1118